**Though he knew it would be good for her to tell the whole story of her kidnapping, he wasn't sure he wanted to hear what she had to say.**

He couldn't afford to let his rage get the better of him.

Dylan eased into the water with Nicole beside him.

"Hold on to me," she said. "I'm afraid…" Her voice trailed off on a sigh.

"I won't let you go. I love you, darlin'." He tightened his grasp around her waist. "Nothing's going to change that."

"Even if I was a coward? If I couldn't get away, get back to you?"

"I should have been there to protect you."

He'd never forgive himself for her pain. He'd never let it happen again.

# CASSIE MILES

# SECLUDED *with the* COWBOY

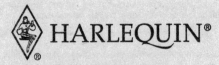

# HARLEQUIN®

TORONTO • NEW YORK • LONDON
AMSTERDAM • PARIS • SYDNEY • HAMBURG
STOCKHOLM • ATHENS • TOKYO • MILAN • MADRID
PRAGUE • WARSAW • BUDAPEST • AUCKLAND

Many, many thanks to Matt Hunsinger-McConnell
for all his editing help.

Recycling programs
for this product may
not exist in your area.

ISBN-13: 978-0-373-69444-0

SECLUDED WITH THE COWBOY

## ABOUT THE AUTHOR

Though born in Chicago and raised in L.A., Cassie Miles has lived in Colorado long enough to be considered a seminative. The first home she owned was a log cabin in the mountains overlooking Elk Creek with a thirty-mile commute to her work at the *Denver Post*.

After raising two daughters and cooking tons of macaroni and cheese for her family, Cassie is trying to be more adventurous in her culinary efforts. Ceviche, anyone? She's discovered that almost anything tastes better with wine. A lot of wine. When she's not plotting Harlequin Intrigue books, Cassie likes to hang out at the Denver Botanical Gardens near her high-rise home.

### Books by Cassie Miles

# CAST OF CHARACTERS

**Nicole Carlisle**—A large-animal veterinarian and ranch wife, she had the strength to endure a brutal kidnapping. But will her marriage survive?

**Dylan Carlisle**—Owner of a vast cattle ranch, he's the ultimate cowboy. After rescuing his wife, he faces an even more lethal threat.

**Maud Applegate**—The local veterinarian is Nicole's mentor and has known her since childhood.

**Nate Miller**—He blames the Carlisle family for the loss of his ranch, his wife and his son. And he wants revenge.

**Lucas Mann**—The foreman at the Carlisle ranch was killed while helping deliver the ransom.

**Sheriff Trainer**—The kidnapping has been almost more than the Delta County sheriff can handle.

**Carolyn Carlisle**—Dylan's older sister can't wait to get back to her CEO duties in Denver.

**J. D. Burke**—The FBI agent stayed behind to deal with the kidnapping and to be with Carolyn.

**Fiona Grant**—The young widow finally feels like she has a real future.

**Jesse Longbridge**—A near-death experience led the professional bodyguard to a fuller life.

**SOF**—Now disbanded, the Sons of Freedom once posed a threat.

*too easy.* The chain leash wasn't long enough for her to reach the rough wooden shelves at the back of the root cellar where Mason jars of preserved peaches, pears, relishes and salsa were stored.

She'd tried to reach those shelves, stretched her legs as far as she could, tried to maneuver the mattress. No luck.

Feeding times were sporadic and unpredictable. Sometimes, he came twice a day with sandwiches and fruit. Today he had appeared once to check on her but hadn't brought food.

Her stomach groaned. *I won't beg for food.*

She'd given up on talking to him. He was deaf to reason. And her threats rang hollow. Nobody was looking for her. Not anymore. Not since she'd been forced to tell her husband that she was safe, that he should call off the search. She'd told him that she was never coming home.

She remembered the pain in Dylan's eyes. They were going through a rough patch in their marriage, and he had believed her when she said she wanted a divorce. *Dammit, he should have known better.* He should have known that she was being coerced.

Three days ago she'd been escorted to her meeting with Dylan by two armed men on horseback. They flanked her as they rode to the creek on Carlisle property. After being held captive, the fresh air and moonlight had been intoxicating. The mountain breeze caressed her cheeks, and she almost began to hope that her ordeal was over. When Dylan rode toward her, looking every inch the cowboy, her heart nearly exploded with longing. It had taken every ounce of self-control to keep herself from leaping into his arms.

But she knew that two rifles were cocked and aimed at her and Dylan. A tiny microphone in her collar broadcast her words to the kidnappers. If she'd deviated from the script, they would both have been killed. She had no other choice but to tell him that their five-year marriage was over.

He'd turned his back. Accepted her at her word.

And she'd been dragged away, transferred from one miserable dungeon to another. This root cellar was the worst. The dank cold permeated her bones. At night the darkness blinded her. Rows of shelves packed with food mocked her hunger.

Overhead, she heard someone walking across the floor. Pipes rattled as the toilet flushed. She'd give a year of her life for the chance to use a bathroom. To take a shower and wash the grit from her blond hair would be pure heaven.

During the first three days after her kidnapping, she'd been allowed to wash up in a basin, to brush her teeth and comb her hair. He'd given her clean clothing so she'd look okay in videos he shot to prove she was still alive. Now that no one was searching, the kidnapper didn't bother to provide her with creature comforts.

Not that Nicole had ever been interested in makeup, powder and perfume. She was a rancher's wife, a veterinarian who didn't require pampering. But she'd always kept herself clean. The stink of her own body humiliated her.

The footsteps crossed the house above her. Though she didn't know the upstairs floorplan, she could tell when he reached the kitchen, which was directly overhead.

Was he bringing her food? Anticipation raced through her, and she hated herself for being excited. *She should be stronger.* A day without food wasn't so long. Logically, she ought to be more concerned about her dwindling water supply. She'd die of dehydration before she starved.

*No! I don't want to die.*

A cry climbed her throat, but there was no point. He'd made sure that no one would hear her. Yesterday… Or was it two days ago? He had prepared her for guests.

He'd said, "We're going to have company, Nicole. I need you to be very quiet. Can you do that?"

"Quiet as a mouse." She'd learned that defiance was futile. Her only chance for survival was to keep him happy.

"If you cooperate, I might let you go."

"Whatever you say." *You bastard. I hate you. Despise you.* "You can trust me."

"And you'll never tell anyone who I am."

He always wore a black ski mask when he came to her, but she knew him. Nate Miller. If she told him that she was aware of his identity, he'd kill her for sure. So she lied, "I don't even know who you are."

As he came closer, her fingers drew into fists. She'd tried to fight him before. He wasn't a big man. Maybe she could knock him down. She could…

"Hold out your hands." From his fingertips, he dangled a keychain—keys to the handcuffs and to the lock that held the chain around her waist. *Was he going to take the cuffs off?* Instead of fighting him, she did as he said.

He looped another chain around the cuffs and shoved her down on the mattress. Then he threw the chain over the ceiling beam and yanked her arms up over her head.

She lashed out with her legs, and he pulled her higher. Her feet no longer touched the ground. Her shoulders throbbed. Her bruised wrists burned with fresh pain.

"I don't trust you," he muttered. "You're still one of

them. You have to pay for all the wrongs the Carlisle family has done to me. It's only fair."

When her arms were secured above her head, he pulled out a roll of duct tape and tore off a piece.

He'd gagged her before. It was terrible. Her throat clogged and she felt as if she couldn't get enough air. She turned her head away, but he was persistent. He slapped the tape over her mouth and left.

Tears coursed down her cheeks as she'd heard people moving in the house—Nate's guests. She'd struggled to cry out, to make some kind of noise. But they'd left, never knowing she was there.

Nate had waited a long time before he came back to the root cellar. Her suspended body had moved beyond pain into numbness. When he released the chain, she'd been too weak to do anything but collapse onto the mattress.

Today—even without food—was a hundred times better.

Overhead, she heard movement again. Someone running.

Something was happening.

She braced herself. Stared at the tiny window beside the rough, heavy door. Time ticked by slowly, and she counted every second. *Please, someone. Please, help me.*

She heard other footsteps in the house. Heavy boots. Several people.

"Help." She screamed with all her might. "I'm down here. Help me."

The force of her cries hammered inside her head, but she kept yelling. Someone had to hear her. Someone had to find her. "Dylan, help me."

PACING ACROSS the kitchen floor, Dylan Carlisle sensed that he was near Nicole. He felt her presence. He imagined that he heard her calling his name, calling from the other side of the hell that had started when she was kidnapped.

The rest of the search party had scattered when they got to the Circle M. Some went to the bunkhouse. Others to the horse barn. They were on the wrong track. *She's here. Close.*

Instinct led him through the back door, down the stairs to the yard. He stood very still, not even breathing, and listened. "Where are you?"

He was answered by a muffled voice. *Her voice, calling for help.*

A tall, thick spruce stood beside the house. Behind that tree he saw concrete steps leading down to a root cellar. He went to the door. Someone was inside, sobbing. "Nicole?"

"Dylan." Her voice was ragged, but it was her. His wife. "Dylan, get me out of here."

He twisted the door handle. Locked, dammit. He couldn't kick the door open; it opened outward instead of pushing in. He unholstered his handgun and aimed at the lock.

"Stand back, Nicole," he said. "I'm going to shoot the lock." Aware that he was probably destroying evidence, he fired into the old door. The wood splintered. He fired again, for good measure, then tore it open on the rusty hinges.

She stood beside a worn-out mattress. Her arms reached toward him. Her face was streaked with grime and tears. She was the most beautiful sight he'd ever seen.

As soon as his arms closed around her, she collapsed.

Gently he sank onto the mattress, holding his wife against his chest. He kissed her forehead. "You're going to be all right. I've got you now."

Through parched lips she whispered, "I'm sorry."

"So am I."

Her eyelids fluttered closed. "Don't let go."

"I won't. Not ever." He snuggled her more tightly against him, belatedly protecting her from the horrors she'd endured. He'd failed her. As a husband and as a man. He could only hope that she'd give him the chance to make things right, to lift her out of this nightmare.

For seven long days he'd feared the worst. He'd gone through every shade of dread and panic.

Finally it was over. He hoped their life would slip back into a regular routine. That was all he'd ever wanted: a simple life on the ranch with Nicole by his side.

His sister, Carolyn, and other members from the search team responded to his gunshots. They poured into the root cellar, and Dylan held Nicole protectively as they brought bottled water for her to drink. The FBI agent who'd stayed behind to help with the search squatted down beside him and expertly picked the locks that fastened the chains and handcuffs.

All the while, Dylan held her. Even with the door wide-open, there wasn't much light in this root cellar. Only one tiny window. At night it must have been total darkness. She'd been trapped, cold and alone. *What kind of bastard could do this to another human being?*

Carolyn tapped his shoulder. "Let's get Nicole out of here."

As he lifted her, she stirred. Her eyes opened. "I want to go home."

"That's where we're headed," he assured her. *Back to normal.* "Back to the ranch."

"Actually," Carolyn said, "we should go to the hospital first. To get you checked out."

Weakly Nicole shook her head. "I want to take a bath first."

"Then that's what we'll do," he said.

A sigh pushed through her chapped lips. Her eyelids drooped shut.

He carried her up the concrete steps into the late-afternoon sunlight. The stairs leading down to the root cellar were well hidden behind the spruce tree. If she hadn't been yelling, they wouldn't have found her so quickly.

The ranch house on the Circle M property wasn't where she'd been kept in the early days of her kidnapping. During their investigation they'd uncovered another hide-out—one that was more pleasant than this filthy dungeon. Apparently Nicole had been shuttled from place to place, always one step ahead of their suspicions.

In the backseat of the SUV, Dylan wrapped her in a wool blanket and arranged her so she was sitting on his lap. She'd lost weight. Her bones felt as fragile as a baby bird's. He whispered, "Don't worry. Everything is going to be fine."

She turned her head to look up at him. Her cheeks were sunken. Smears of grit stood out against her pale skin, and dark circles ringed her eyes. "Do you mean that, Dylan? Everything?"

Before she was abducted, they'd argued. He never wanted to fight with her again. "It's going to be exactly the way you want it."

Carolyn started the engine and pulled up the long drive that led to the main road. "She needs medical attention, Dylan. Does Nicole have a regular doctor I can call?"

Only the specialists at the fertility clinic, and he wasn't about to call those jerks. "I don't know her doctor's name."

"I'll contact Doc Maud."

"Great idea," he muttered. "Except for one thing. Maud is a veterinarian."

"She'll know other doctors. People doctors."

Any old doctor wasn't good enough. He wanted his wife to have the best of care. For too long he'd taken her for granted, hadn't appreciated her.

"I'll make the call," Carolyn said, waving her cell phone.

"Back off. I'll do it." His sister's take-charge attitude irritated him. Though she was only two years older than he was, Carolyn insisted on being the boss, especially after their dad had passed away five years ago. Dylan would be glad when she went back to running the Denver offices of Carlisle Certified Organic Beef. Carolyn belonged in the city.

And he belonged at the ranch where he managed two thousand head of grass-fed, antibiotic-free Black Angus. Before the kidnapping they'd had a pretty good life. A couple of bumps in the road but nothing serious. He and Nicole could be happy again. Maybe even better than before.

Through the window he watched the golden sunset spread above distant snow-capped peaks. Nicole loved these Colorado skies. When they got married, they promised to share every sunset. They'd even engraved that vow on their wedding bands with the words, "My horizon." She was his promise, his hope, his final destination.

He looked down into her eyes. Her lips were unsmiling. "Those things I said, about wanting a divorce…"

"It's okay," he said. "You don't have to explain."

"If I hadn't said that, we both would have been shot." She swallowed hard. "There were two of them with rifles aimed at both of us. And that wasn't all. If I had escaped, Nate said he'd go on a rampage. Kill my horses. The barn cats. Every person connected to Carlisle Ranch would suffer."

In retrospect, Dylan realized that he should have guessed that she'd been forced to say what she did. But Nicole had been damn convincing. Looked him straight in the eye and told him that their marriage was over.

For the past several weeks they'd been arguing. She'd accused him of not listening to her, and that he paid too much attention to running the ranch and not enough to their relationship. She'd been angry at him. That was for damn sure.

But she'd never once said she didn't love him or that she wanted a divorce. Those were Nate Miller's words. And when Nicole spoke them, they were bullets to Dylan's heart.

In that moment he'd wanted to die. Losing her to a kidnapper was hell. Losing her because she didn't want to be with him was even worse.

Determinedly, he said, "We're going to be okay."

"Know what I've been dreaming about? What I really want?"

"Tell me."

"An energy bar with peanuts and raisins."

Dylan stroked dank strands of hair off her forehead. "You always liked those granola bars."

Her predictability pleased him. *Back to normal. Everything is going to be all right.*

## Chapter Two

When her husband escorted her across the threshold of their upstairs bedroom at the ranch house, a strong sense of familiarity overwhelmed Nicole. Surrounded by memories, she truly felt that she was home. And safe.

Every detail—from the green-sprigged wallpaper to the sandy wall-to-wall carpet—matched her personal taste. She'd selected the dark oak furniture. The cream-colored duvet and the pillows plumped up against the headboard promised a comfortable sleep.

Her gaze caught on the framed family photos displayed above the dresser, and she reached toward their wedding picture. In his tuxedo with his black hair combed, Dylan was tall, dashing and gallant. Standing beside him, she looked tiny in her lacy white gown. Though she'd been wearing three-inch heels to enhance her five-foot-two inch height, the top of her head still didn't reach higher than his chin. "Our wedding. I was so happy."

Dylan smiled. "Best day of my life."

Her hand touching the photo was filthy. So much had changed. The bumps and bruises she'd been trying to ignore ached. Her whole body felt sore.

She staggered into the adjoining bathroom and turned

on the faucet in the sink. The grime and stench of captivity disgusted her. She needed to be clean again.

After she'd washed her hands and face, she confronted her reflection in the mirror above the sink. She leaned close. "I look awful."

"Not to me." Dylan handed her a towel and gently rested his hand on her shoulder. "It's like I always said. No matter where you are, no matter what you do, you're always the most beautiful woman in the room."

"I'm the only woman in this bathroom," she pointed out.

"So I'm not lying."

It was good to see him smile. He had obviously suffered in her absence. The strain showed in the deepening of the lines at the corners of his pale green eyes. His usually ruddy complexion had paled. "This was hard on you."

"I kept thinking I'd never see you again, never hear your voice, never…" He choked off his words before getting emotional. Dylan wasn't the sort of man who put his feelings on display. "I'll be glad when things get back to normal."

There was a knock at their bedroom door, and he went to answer. She heard Carolyn's voice and Dylan's response as he said they wanted to be alone.

Nicole appreciated his concern for her privacy. Though she didn't feel completely wiped out, she needed some time to pull herself together and to heal. She heard Carolyn mention Dylan's mother, Andrea. Was she here? Had Andrea come to the ranch? If so, Nicole would be surprised. Dylan and his mother had been estranged for years.

He closed the bedroom door and carried a tray laden with three energy bars, a ham-and-cheese sandwich and a mug of milk. To her eye, the simple repast looked like a feast. As soon as he set the tray down on the table by the window, she pounced on an energy bar, tore off the wrapper and took a bite. Never had anything tasted so fabulous. She chased the granola with a sip of milk. "Omigod. Omigod."

Dylan laughed. "Hungry?"

"I guess so." She lowered herself into the padded rocking chair beside the table, glad that the cushion was forest-green and wouldn't show the dirt from her jeans. "My bath is going to wait until I have some food."

Another bite of granola. Another swig of milk. She picked up the sandwich. The homemade bread felt heavy and healthy. The ham, the yellow American cheese and the crisp lettuce had her taste buds exploding in ecstasy. Though she fully intended to devour the whole thing, she was full after only three or four bites.

Leaning back in the rocking chair, she sipped the milk. "Did Carolyn say something about your mom?"

"Andrea's here," he said coldly. His mother had divorced Dylan's father and moved to Manhattan when Dylan was only five years old. "I didn't invite her."

No surprise. He'd never forgiven his mother for leaving, despite the obvious fact that Andrea was a city woman. And she was happy in New York. Years ago she'd remarried and had another child—a half sister that Dylan had never met. "Why is she here?"

"Carolyn called and told her you'd been kidnapped. Andrea took it upon herself to come out here. A waste of time."

"Don't be hard on her. She wanted to offer support."

"Too late for that."

Nicole recognized certain unfortunate parallels between Dylan's mother and herself. They both had married strong-willed ranchers. Dylan's father, Sterling Carlisle, had a reputation for being tough, demanding and ambitious. In the late 1980s he'd changed his ranching methods to organic before that became the thing to do. Sterling had established a family empire that had grown into a multimillion-dollar business. But there had been a personal cost. He'd made a lot of enemies. And his intense focus on the ranch might have left Andrea feeling isolated and abandoned. Nicole knew how it felt to be ignored while Dylan tended to business.

"I'm glad your mother is here," she said. "The only other time I've seen her was at our wedding, but I've kept in touch. You know, with Christmas cards and e-mails. Family is important, Dylan."

"I know." A muscle in his jaw twitched, and she guessed that he was holding back a hostile comment about his mother.

"I still miss my parents." She'd been an only child, adopted by parents who were older, both in their late forties when she was an infant. Both had passed away before her twenty-first birthday. "I never had any other relatives."

"You've got me." He stood by the rocking chair and took her hand. "You're everything to me. My family. My partner. My friend. My lover."

In spite of her aches and pains, she wanted to be in his arms, to replace her memories of captivity with sweet intimacy. She wanted his kisses, wanted to feel…wanted. Yet, when he leaned closer, she pushed him away. "Not yet. I'm too gross. I need to take my bath."

"I can wait."

She rose from the rocking chair, grabbed another

energy bar and moved toward the bathroom. "This might take a long time."

"Need any help?"

His offer was tempting, but she refused. Her plan was to shower first and wash her hair, four or five times. Then she'd soak until every pore of her body was clean.

He stood in the bathroom doorway. "I'll be waiting out here until you're done."

She started the shower. After she stripped off the clothes she'd worn for so many days, she opened the door and tossed them out. "I never want to see these again."

"They're gone," Dylan said.

She closed the door again, grateful to be home and in control of her life. Naked, she stepped into the shower. The hot water sluiced down her body, washing away the top layer of grime. With a washcloth she scrubbed hard, hoping to erase the horror and humiliation. *Will I ever be clean again?*

Nate had forced her to do things she never wanted to do—to look at her husband in the eye and tell him she wanted a divorce. *She'd had no choice.* If she'd disobeyed, they would both be dead.

Dylan understood. He didn't blame her for what she'd done. Her tears mingled with the pelting water of the shower. She needed more time to forgive herself.

A FEW HOURS LATER, Dylan woke from the best sleep he'd had in seven days with Nicole snuggled up beside him on the bed. After her soak in the tub, her skin smelled like spring flowers. Her blond hair was still damp. When he nestled her small body against him, his heart swelled. She'd come back to him, back to where she belonged.

He hadn't planned to fall asleep on their bed while she was in the bathroom, but once he'd stretched out on top of the covers, he faded fast. During the whole time she'd been kidnapped, he hadn't once slept in their bed. He couldn't. Not until she was beside him.

"Nicole," he whispered. "Darlin', are you awake?"

Her breathing was slow and steady, indicating the kind of deep sleep that came from sheer exhaustion.

He noticed that she'd left the bedside lamp burning, which was odd. Usually she blocked out every glimmer of light before going to bed. Being held in that dank root cellar must have made her think differently about the darkness.

Her fingers curled loosely below her chin. He noticed the bruises at her wrists where the handcuffs had been. Seeing those marks infuriated him. He eased the sleeve of her nightgown higher up her arm, revealing more black and blue skin. *Damn Nate Miller.* The son of a bitch had escaped.

Dylan glanced at the bedside clock. It was only a few minutes past eleven o'clock. While Nicole was sleeping, he could slip downstairs and find out what was happening with the ongoing investigation into Nate's whereabouts.

Leaving the bed, he tucked the covers up to her chin. She didn't stir. Not a bit. Not even when he kissed the tip of her nose. His wife was an angel from heaven. And Nate deserved the tortures of hell for what he'd done to her.

Downstairs, he found his sister and FBI agent J. D. Burke sitting side by side at the dining-room table, staring at a computer screen. Burke had been the first federal agent on the scene when Carolyn called in the FBI to investigate the kidnapping. The rest of the FBI team had left after the ransom was paid, but he'd stayed—mostly because of his unexpected relationship with Carolyn. Burke wanted to marry her, God help him.

Carolyn stood. "How's Nicole?"

"Sleeping. She doesn't seem to be in bad shape, but it's hard to tell." He thought of the bruises and winced. "She's never been a whiner."

"I'm telling you," Carolyn said. "She needs to be checked out by a doctor."

"And if that's what Nicole wants, I'll drive her to the hospital." He looked toward Burke. "What happened with Nate?"

"He's gone." Burke stood and stretched. He was a big man—a bit taller than Dylan and a lot heavier, all of it solid muscle. "When I'm done with this case, I will never again undertake another investigation in the mountains. People disappear around here like thistles on the wind."

"You're exaggerating," Carolyn said. "People can hide in the city, too."

"But cities have surveillance cameras. And other people who can give information." He glowered. "The only eyewitnesses around here are the nighthawks and the cattle."

"I want him found," Dylan said. "I won't rest easy until Nate Miller is either dead or behind bars."

Burke turned the computer toward him. On the screen was a map of the area. "We've been trying to figure out where to look. Sheriff Trainer and his men are keeping an eye on Nate's little house in Riverton. And a couple of other deputies are posted at the Circle M in case he returns there."

"We should get the FBI back here," Dylan said. "With surveillance choppers and sniffer dogs."

"We tried that when we were first looking for Nicole," Burke pointed out. "Not a real successful tactic."

Though Dylan had grown up at the ranch and was familiar with this land, they were dealing with thousands of acres—much of it heavily forested. "Seems like the only person who's had any luck with tracking is Jesse Longbridge."

"Luck is what we need," Carolyn said. "The forecast for tomorrow is snow."

Snowfall and freezing temperatures would drive Nate out of hiding. "Do you think he'll stay in this area?"

"It's not logical for him to stick around," Burke said. "Jesse and Fiona recovered most of the million-dollar ransom when they finally tracked down Pete Richter at Nate's house, but there's still over a hundred thousand missing. That's enough money for Nate to start a new life somewhere else."

But he had strong ties to this area. He'd lived here all his life, and his four-year-old son was here. Surely he'd never see the boy again. Nate's ex-wife wouldn't allow him to be get within a hundred yards of their child.

"If he goes somewhere else," Dylan said, "how will we find him?"

"Nate's in the law enforcement system now. There's a warrant out for his arrest. And an APB. Any cop who sees him will pick him up."

"And if he isn't picked up?"

Burke lifted his coffee mug to his mouth and took a sip. "A lot of lawbreakers are never apprehended."

Too easily, Dylan imagined Nate changing his name and hiring on as a handyman or cowboy at a ranch somewhere far away. Most ranchers weren't particular about job history when they hired a new hand, and Nate had skills. In addition to ranching, he'd been working as a handyman for years. "He might get away with this."

"It's too bad Nicole's asleep," Carolyn said. "If Nate's around here, she might have some idea where he's hiding."

"Nobody is going to question her." Dylan was firm on this point. "She's suffered enough. It's best for her to just forget about what happened."

"*If* she can forget," Burke said. "That's a big if."

"What do you mean?"

"I'm not a profiler, but I know a thing or two about victims of violent crimes. It's important for people who've gone through trauma to tell their stories."

"I agree," his sister said.

"Of course you do," Dylan muttered.

Carolyn always complained about how cowboys kept their feelings bottled up. She'd rather have them sit around the campfire and have group therapy. "Nicole needs to talk about what happened."

She reached up and tightened her ponytail. Her coloring, with black hair and green eyes, was the same as his. She was tall and lean, like him. The two of them looked like the male and female version of the same DNA pattern. They were both stubborn and competitive, constantly butting heads.

"I don't want you interrogating her," Dylan said. "Either of you."

"Even if it's for the best?" Carolyn asked.

"I'll decide what's best for my wife."

He heard a soft footstep behind him and turned. Nicole, wearing a navy blue velour robe, stood behind him. "Actually," she said, "I'll make that decision."

He wrapped an arm around her and escorted her to a

chair. "I don't want you to be pressured. Your only job is to get well."

When she looked up at him, her gaze was sharp and determined. "Here's what I want," she said. "Nate Miller in jail."

"We're on the same page," he said.

"If there's any way I can help put him there, I'm ready." She looked at Burke. "Ask your questions."

## Chapter Three

Moments ago Nicole had wakened from a nightmare, sitting up on her bed. Her neck arched. Her mouth stretched open, wide-open, as if to scream in terror. Only a tiny moan escaped.

*No one can hear me.*

She knew that wasn't true. She was free. And yet her eyes darted wildly. The room was hazy. The wallpaper faded into concrete walls. She looked down at her hands. Though she wasn't bound, she couldn't pull her wrists apart. Invisible handcuffs held her.

"No," she whispered. She was at home in her own soft, comfortable bed. She was warm, clean and safe. Alone.

*No one can see me.*

Concentrating, she struggled to control the rapid beating of her heart. She forced her wrists to separate. With one arm on each side of her body, she lay back on the pillows. Her body went stiff. Frozen, she waited for the panic to subside.

Her stomach churned. She bolted from the bed, raced to the bathroom and vomited. Her eyes avoided the mirror as she rinsed her mouth and brushed her teeth. *Coward!* She didn't want to see the self-doubt in her eyes, didn't want to confront the fear that caused her heart to throb inside her rib cage.

She could pretend that she was all right, but it was a lie. Until Nate was caught, she was shackled inside her own terror.

Looking back at the bed, she knew going back to sleep was out of the question. Though Dylan had promised to stay with her, she was kind of glad that he hadn't. She didn't want him to see her fall apart.

Pulling on her robe and slippers, she went downstairs where she heard Dylan talking to Carolyn and that big, tall FBI agent with the dark, piercing eyes. They were making plans to catch Nate, and she could help.

Dylan sat beside her at the dining-room table. "You don't have to do this, Nicole."

"I can handle it." If she ever wanted to rest easy, she needed to know that Nate was behind bars. She looked toward the FBI agent. "I don't believe we've been introduced."

Carolyn rested her hand on the man's broad shoulder. "This is Agent J. D. Burke. Otherwise known as my fiancé."

That was a shocker. Carolyn hadn't been serious about anyone in years. "Congratulations."

"They're a good match," Dylan said with a wry smile. "Burke's the only man I've ever met who just might be tough enough to handle my sister."

Ignoring her brother, Carolyn turned to Nicole. "Can I get you anything to eat or drink? Coffee?"

"Herbal tea," she said. Something to soothe her stomach. "Chamomile with honey. The teabags are on the second shelf—"

"I know where to find the tea."

Never before had Nicole seen her sister-in-law prepare any sort of food or drink. "Don't tell me you're learning how to cook."

"I can zap water in the microwave." She glared at Burke, who was doing his best not to smirk. "Don't get any ideas. I'm not about to turn domesticated."

"The thought never crossed my mind." Burke watched as she stalked toward the kitchen, then he took a seat at the head of the table, directly to Nicole's right. In a calm but authoritative voice he said, "I'm not going to pressure you. My questions will help figure out Nate's behavior patterns so we can predict what he'll do next."

"FBI profiling," she said.

"How do you know about—"

"I watch TV."

"Then you know what I want," Burke said with a grin. "Why don't you start at the beginning? Tell us about the day you were kidnapped."

Nicole exhaled a long sigh, remembering that day. They'd been having trouble at the ranch—incidents of sabotage in the south field had culminated in a fire that burned down the old stable. Dylan had hired Longbridge Security to keep an eye on things, but tensions were still high.

"Jesse Longbridge warned me not to go off by myself. If I wanted to take a ride, I was supposed to let him or one of the other bodyguards know."

But she'd been angry. Dylan had been trying to weasel out of an appointment at the fertility clinic the following day because he claimed that he needed to be at the ranch until all this sabotage was straightened out. For eight months they'd been trying to get pregnant, and the timing of this appointment was crucial. How could he refuse? It seemed as if he just didn't care about having a baby.

"I broke Jesse's rule," she said. "I needed some time alone. So I went to the barn, saddled up and rode. I headed toward the creek near the south pasture."

She'd dismounted and gone to the water's edge. Her teeming emotions had blinded her to the approaching danger. She hadn't seen the two men lurking in the trees. "The man who grabbed me was Sam Logan—the leader of the Sons of Freedom. They're that cult that rented the Circle M from Nate to set up their compound."

"We know," Burke said.

"I didn't recognize the other guy, but I later learned that his name was Pete Richter. I struggled. One of them hit me. Everything went black."

"Do you remember gunshots?" Burke asked.

"Was someone hurt?"

Dylan cleared his throat and took her hand. The grave expression in his eyes told her that bad news was coming. "Jesse went after you. He was shot, and was in a coma for a couple of days. But he's better now."

"A coma…" His injury was her fault. If she hadn't gone running off by herself, none of this would have happened.

"Don't beat yourself up," Carolyn said as she returned to the dining room with Nicole's herbal tea. "Nobody blames you."

"But I—"

"Jesse's a professional bodyguard. When he got shot, he was doing his job," Carolyn said. "Besides, he's definitely recovered. He's better than ever."

"What do you mean?"

Carolyn placed the steaming mug on the table in

front of her. "There might be wedding bells in the future for Jesse and our neighbor, Fiona Grant."

Nicole's burden of guilt lifted. She wasn't surprised that Fiona, a young widow, had found love with the handsome bodyguard. "First you and Burke. Then Jesse and Fiona."

Carolyn chuckled as she plopped into a chair on the opposite side of the table. "That's right."

"Jeez." Nicole shook her head. "I get myself kidnapped for a week and come back to find everybody coupled up. Are you going to have a double wedding?"

"Not a chance," Dylan said. "Carolyn's not about to share that spotlight."

Burke drummed his fingers on the tabletop. "Let's get back to your story, Nicole. What's the next thing you remember?"

She sipped her chamomile tea. She would have preferred gossiping about these newly formed couples, but she knew it was important to talk about what happened. "Maybe I should just skip ahead to when Nate showed up."

"Let's keep going in order," Burke said. "You were with Logan and Richter."

"They took me to the Circle M. I was only stunned for a couple of minutes." She remembered checking herself for injuries. Her father had been a doctor, and she knew that head injuries could be dangerous. If she'd had a concussion, it was minor. "We left the Circle M almost immediately. My hands were tied in front of me. I was blindfolded and gagged."

"How were you transported?" Burke asked.

"On horseback. There were two guys. Richter and Thurgood. Much as I hate to give those kidnappers credit for anything, Butch Thurgood was a good horseman. He held me in front of him on the saddle."

"He was a former rodeo star," Carolyn informed her.

"Well, he did a good job of controlling me and his horse at the same time. We headed up the Indian trail that starts near the south pasture and leads to the pass."

"And they took you to a cave," Carolyn prompted.

"That's right."

"Carolyn," Dylan said in a warning tone. "This is Nicole's story. Let her talk."

Nicole continued, "We stopped at a high cave overlooking the trail. I was hoping and praying that nobody would come after us. Butch and Richter had the perfect vantage point. I could tell they'd been there before when they set up camp. I figured it was something to do with the Sons of Freedom."

She paused, realizing that she'd missed a lot while she'd been held captive. "What happened to the SOF, anyway? When Nate took me to the Circle M, we were alone."

Burke explained, "The SOF was part of a network of survivalist groups that was smuggling guns and drugs. We mounted a major FBI operation to take them out. All the women and children were rescued. The men are in custody, including Sam Logan."

"What about their horses?" she asked. "They had eight or ten at the Circle M. And two Arabians."

"We'll make sure they're taken care of," Dylan said. "I'll send a couple of hands over in the morning."

Her kidnapping had set off a wide-ranging course of events. A major FBI operation? Women and children rescued? "When did all this happen?"

Dylan leaned toward her. "Everything happened at the same time. Nate must have planned it that way for maximum confusion."

"How did he know the timing?" she asked.

"He had an informant. Someone who betrayed us," Dylan said darkly. "So while the FBI closed in on the SOF, Carolyn and I had our instructions. She went to deliver the ransom, and I rode to meet you at the creek."

She glanced toward him, half expecting to see reproach. Instead, his gaze was steady and calm. For once in his life, Dylan seemed completely nonjudgmental. He wouldn't growl and tell her that she'd made a mess of things.

He was her anchor. Lacing her fingers through his, she clung to him.

"I'm confused," Carolyn said. "You were abducted by the guys from the SOF. How did you end up with Nate Miller?"

"At the cave." She continued to gaze into Dylan's cool green eyes. "They fell asleep, and I tried to escape. My hands were still tied, but I managed to get the ropes off my ankles. I climbed down the side of the cliff. And I ran right into the waiting arms of Nate Miller."

"Ouch," Carolyn said. "Talk about jumping from the frying pan into the fire."

"I thought he'd help me. He was wearing a black ski mask, which I thought was a little strange, but the night was chilly."

"How did you know it was Nate?" Burke asked.

"I know how," Dylan said. "She recognized his horse."

She nodded. "I'm a vet. I know livestock better than people. I've never treated Nate's horse, but I've seen him plenty of times in that little corral in Riverton. I worried that the animal wasn't getting enough exercise."

"You went quietly with Nate," Burke said.

"That's right. I climbed up on the saddle and rode

with him. I didn't bother with untying my hands because I wanted to put distance between us and the kidnappers."

"And you rode to Fiona Grant's property," Burke said.

"Nate told me we were supposed to wait inside the barn. That's when he took out his gun."

And she'd realized how foolish she'd been to trust him. "He ordered me to climb down into a little room hidden under the floor. He left my hands tied and used a shackle on my ankle to tether me to the bed frame. Then he left. I was alone."

*No one could help me.* That little cell under the barn floor wasn't badly furnished. The single bed was fairly comfortable. There was light from a lamp beside the bed. The walls and ceiling were insulated, so it was fairly warm. "That's when it hit me. I might not get out of this mess alive. I had time to think. And I was scared."

Dylan reached toward her, but she pulled away. Part of her wanted to curl up in his arms and sob. She wanted the warm reassurance of his love. But not right now. "I need to keep going, Dylan. I might remember something useful, something that will help catch Nate."

"Did he talk to you?" Burke asked.

She nodded. "He used a whispery voice. As if I didn't already know who he was. I played along. It seemed prudent to pretend I didn't know his identity."

"Smart move," Burke said. "It might have saved your life. Did he mention any specifics?"

She concentrated, trying to recall through the miasma of fear and frustration that colored her time in captivity. "Mostly he talked about how much he hated the Carlisles. He blames us for every bad thing that's happened to him. Losing his herd. The failure of his marriage."

"Sounds like he's obsessed," Burke said.

"Exactly." She nodded. "If he catches the sniffles, he's pretty sure that the Carlisles infected him."

"What else do you remember?"

"Threats. He told me that if I didn't cooperate, he'd destroy everything I cared about. He'd wreak havoc. Kill the people and the animals I love. Burn down the buildings." An involuntary shudder rippled through her. "And he sounded like he'd relish every minute."

"His hatred gives him a reason to stay in this area," Burke said. "The rational course of action would be to run."

"He's not rational." But he was exceedingly clever. Though he hadn't planned the kidnapping, he'd taken advantage of the situation. He must have followed Butch and Richter when they took her to the cave. As soon as their backs were turned, he'd grabbed her.

"Tell us about when he made those proof-of-life videotapes."

She turned to Dylan. "I tried to signal you with a clue to his identity. I kept making the sign of the Circle M— Nate's ranch."

"We noticed," Carolyn said. "But we misinterpreted the meaning. We thought your clues about Circle M referred to the SOF. They were the ones living at the ranch."

She groaned. "That makes perfect sense."

"Did you have any further contact with Butch and Richter?" Burke asked.

"They were the ones holding me when I met with Dylan by the creek. Both of them had rifles in their hands and were ready to shoot."

"They partnered up with Nate," Carolyn said. "Why would they do that after he double-crossed them? He snatched you away from them at the caves."

"He must have promised them a share in the ransom," Burke said.

Nicole shuddered. Nate had a way of getting people to do what he wanted. "Butch didn't seem like such a bad guy. If it had only been him, I might have tried to escape. But Richter was mean."

"You have no idea," Carolyn said. "He was stalking Fiona, trying to get his hands on that damned ransom."

"What happened to him?"

"He's in custody," Burke said.

"And Butch?"

"He was murdered by Richter."

Butch was dead. Jesse had been seriously injured. The violence depressed her. And she knew it wasn't over. As long as Nate was at large, there would be more carnage.

Burke asked, "What happened after you talked to Dylan?"

"Everything got confused. They locked me in the trunk of a car. I tried to pay attention and figure out where we were going."

"What did you notice?" Burke asked.

"The smell. I think we stopped at the gas station in Riverton. Silas O'Toole's place."

"Did you hear anything?"

"Not until Nate came. He drove the car to his little house in Riverton and marched me inside. I was locked up in his closet. Gagged the whole time."

The only positive thing about being stuck in a closet was that he let her come out and use the bathroom while he stood guard, gun in hand.

"After a day and a half, he took me back to the Circle M's root cellar."

"When you were at his house," Burke said, "did you hear anything through the door?"

"I heard him on the phone." She remembered his plain, ugly house. "He had toys for his son. A shiny red tricycle in the middle of the living room. And a new cowboy hat. Maybe they were supposed to be Christmas presents."

"Did he mention his son?"

"He never spoke the child's name, but he did talk about how sons need their fathers." She remembered the whispery voice, eerie and creepy. "'A boy needs someone to show him how to be a man.' He said that more than once."

Carolyn shuddered. "Is someone keeping an eye on Nate's ex-wife and son?"

"Don't worry. The sheriff is making sure that Belinda Miller is well protected." Burke leaned forward. "Maintaining contact with his son gives Nate another reason to stay in this area."

"I think we've got our answer about what Nate's going to do next," Dylan said. "He's got a vendetta against us. He won't quit until he gets even."

"What do we do?"

"We wait," Burke said. "It won't be long. He's got to be enraged about Nicole's rescue. He'll want to take action."

Nicole didn't want to think about Nate creeping around their property, hiding in the forests, biding his time. He was desperate for revenge. Somebody was going to get hurt.

# Chapter Four

As soon as she and Dylan returned to the bedroom, Nicole's self-control began to crumble. She'd managed to tell the story of her kidnapping in broad strokes, leaving out the humiliating details. How could she ever speak of those things? The filth. Her screams into empty darkness. Her gnawing hunger.

It was better to bury those horrors under layers of silence, not telling even Dylan. *Especially not Dylan.* When he looked at her, she didn't want him to see a victim—a helpless, terrified creature.

She sat on the edge of her bed, hands folded in her lap, hating the unassuaged fear that roiled inside her. Desperately she longed to forget the kidnapping, to erase every scrap of it from her memory.

Dylan sat beside her and wrapped his arm around her, cradling her with unusual tenderness, as if afraid that she'd shatter if he held her too tightly. Leaning her cheek against his chest, she whispered, "I don't want to fall asleep."

"Nightmares?"

"If I let my defenses down, I remember too much." Her breath shuddered. "I might lose control."

"You're safe now, darlin'." He stroked her hair. "You know I'll take care of you. It's going to be all right."

Much as she wanted to believe him, her fears would not be so easily cured. Her nostrils flared as she remembered the stink of the dank, dark places where she'd been held captive.

In the creaking of the old ranch house, she heard echoes of mocking laughter. "Why does Nate hate us so much?"

Dylan tightened his embrace. His muscles tensed. "When I think of what that bastard did to you…" He exhaled slowly, forcing himself to relax. "I won't let him hurt you. Not ever again."

Downstairs, the front door slammed hard enough that they could hear it all the way up here in their bedroom. It sounded as if a herd of buffalo had charged inside. Someone called out Dylan's name.

"I'd better see what they need," Dylan said.

She understood that he was the boss, and the Carlisle Ranch was his responsibility. But she wanted his full attention tonight. When he stood, she rose to her feet beside him. "I'm coming with you."

"It's okay," he said. "You can rest."

"Didn't I just tell you that I don't want to sleep? You never listen to me." The familiar complaint sparked her anger. "Have you heard one word I've said?"

"I get it." He glanced toward the door. "If you want me to stay here with you, that's what I'll do."

She didn't want to argue. "Go. But I'm coming with you."

"Yes, ma'am."

Together they went down the hallway and stood side by side on the staircase, looking down at two ranch hands in gloves, cowboy hats and heavy jackets. Both wore guns on their hips. Both were out of breath.

"What's up?" Dylan asked.

"Somebody cut the barbed wire on the south pasture. We got cattle running loose."

Dylan's tone was clipped. "Rouse anybody who's sleeping in the bunkhouse and get on it."

"What about the men who are standing guard?"

"They stay put," he said. "The house needs to be secure."

"Okay, boss."

"You boys get started. I'll be with you in a minute." As the ranch hands went out the door, Dylan turned to her. "I need to see to this problem."

"No," she said.

He took her hand. "I'll get Carolyn to stay with you. This shouldn't be a big deal, and I—"

"You can't go," she said. "Cut wires on the south pasture? That's deliberate sabotage. Remember what Burke said about Nate staying in this area until he takes his revenge? He cut that fence."

"I reckon you're right. But there's close to three hundred cattle in the south field. I need to help."

"Nate's baiting you, trying to draw you outside." She reached up and touched his cheek. "Please, stay here with me."

"I'm not hiding from Nate Miller."

His green eyes darkened. She'd always loved the clarity she saw in his gaze. Though Dylan was good at disguising the way he felt, his eyes were truly windows to his soul. She saw his determination, fire and strength. She knew that he was ready to go into battle. My God, he was handsome. Her husband stood ready to protect her, to fight for her.

But right now she didn't need a hero. "Listen to me. Please listen. If anything happens to you—"

"I can take care of myself." His smile was fierce. "I'd welcome a showdown with that sorry son of a bitch."

He made it sound as if this would be a fair fight, like a duel, with the two of them facing off. "Nate could be hiding in the forest with a rifle. He could pick you off before you know what's happening. You could be dead before you have a chance to draw your gun."

He leaned down and lightly kissed her forehead. "I'll be back before you know it."

As he descended the staircase, she watched. She was proud of his courage. But furious at the same time. Even now, after everything she'd been through, he brushed her warning aside. "Stubborn," she muttered under her breath.

After blowing her a kiss, he strode out the door, plunging headlong into danger. She sank down on the staircase and slumped forward, exhausted. But she knew she wouldn't sleep. Not while Dylan was in jeopardy.

From behind her, a gentle voice offered, "Shall I make tea?"

She turned her head and looked up at Andrea, Dylan's mother—a woman she barely knew. Nicole stood on the stair and adjusted her robe. Politely, she said, "It's nice to see you."

In a mauve kimono-style robe with a striped pattern at the sleeves and hem, Andrea looked big-city sophisticated, even without makeup. She pulled Nicole into a hug. "Thank God you're all right. I was so worried."

"Thanks, Andrea."

"I should be thanking you." She linked arms with

Nicole and descended the staircase. "Until you came along, I'd pretty much lost contact with my son. You have no idea how much I appreciate the Christmas cards and birthday greetings that you send."

Nicole hadn't made a special effort. Keeping in touch with Andrea simply seemed like the right thing to do. "We're family. Staying in touch is important."

"I especially like the photos. My daughter in New York would love to come out here for a visit."

"She's welcome anytime."

They entered the kitchen just as Carolyn and Burke stumbled out from the pantry. From the disheveled state of their clothing and their sheepish expressions, it was pretty obvious why they hadn't run to answer the front door.

"What's going on?" Carolyn demanded.

Her mother answered, "Some fencing was cut on the south pasture. Sabotage."

"It's got to be Nate Miller," Burke said.

"Dylan has already gone running out there to help round up the cattle." Andrea's tone was authoritative. "I would appreciate it, Burke, if you went along to keep an eye on him. Carolyn, you stay here."

"Why?" Carolyn was never one to accept orders without question.

Nicole said, "Because Nate wants revenge against the Carlisles. *The whole family.* You'd be a target."

"She's right," Burke said, giving her a quick kiss. "I'll take care of this. Maybe I can get your brother to put on a Kevlar vest."

"Please do," Nicole said. "A suit of body armor would be great."

If anything happened to Dylan, she didn't think she

could stand it. He was stubborn, inattentive and arrogant. But he was still her husband.

DYLAN RODE with Burke across the field behind the horse barn toward the south pasture—a fenced area that had been the site of prior sabotage before Nicole was kidnapped. His schedule of rotating the two thousand head of Carlisle cattle on land they owned and land they leased had gotten out of whack. Now that Nicole was home, he could get back to the serious business of ranching. It wasn't going to be easy. His foreman, Lucas Mann, had been killed when the ransom was delivered.

Thinking of that death, he cringed inside, still unable to believe that Lucas—a trusted employee of many years—had betrayed the family by helping the Sons of Freedom. Nicole would be heartbroken when he told her. She'd probably insist on handling the funeral in spite of Lucas's treachery.

Dylan scanned the familiar terrain. The night had gotten cold. A brisk wind chased clouds across the moon in a portent of the snowfall that was predicted for tomorrow. He slowed his horse to a walk. From here, they could cut through the forest where—as Nicole had suggested— Nate Miller could be hiding with his rifle. That was the route Dylan wanted to take; he wanted a confrontation.

"This way," he said to Burke.

"We should stick to the road."

"I like the trees." He tugged at the uncomfortable bulletproof vest Burke insisted he wear.

"You like the idea of finding Nate and getting into a shoot-out," Burke said. "Can't say that I blame you. But if you get yourself shot, Carolyn will kick my butt. That's why we need to take the safer route."

After a longing glance toward the dark forest, Dylan conceded and turned toward the road. "Let's suppose that Nate cut the fence to draw me out here, and he's planning an ambush."

"Damn likely scenario," Burke muttered.

"What's the best way to handle it?"

"Do the opposite of what seems natural."

"The opposite?" If Dylan hadn't respected Burke's talent for strategy, he would have laughed out loud. "You're going to have to explain."

"An ambush is a lure," Burke said. "You're Nate's target. He wants to make you come to him."

"So if I see the flash of gunfire or hear a shot, I shouldn't respond by riding toward it."

"Right," Burke said. "Because that's what he expects you to do."

"I should back down." He hated the idea, but it made sense. "Our advantage is in numbers. There are a lot of us and only one of him. We should go after him carefully. Make sure we cut off his escape."

"You got it," Burke said.

They approached the far edge of the field, close to Fiona Grant's property. Not only had the barbed wire been cut, but the fencing was peeled back between two posts, allowing the cattle an easy exit.

Tomorrow morning, a portion of this herd was destined to be removed to the slaughterhouse in Delta, and these Black Angus cattle seemed to anticipate their fate. There was a lot of bawling, as if the animals were encouraging each other to make a break. More than fifty had already ambled through the gap in the fence and were moving down the road.

Dylan was surprised to see Jesse Longbridge helping

his cowboys round up the cattle. Jesse was staying at Fiona's house to protect her and her five-year-old daughter. He rode toward them and reined his horse. "What the hell are you doing out here, Dylan?"

"Ranching. This is my business."

"My business is keeping you safe," he said. "Don't make my job harder. I'll escort you back to the house."

"That's not going to happen." Never in his life had Dylan run from a fight. "Shouldn't you be keeping an eye on Fiona and her little girl?"

"One of my men is at her house, making sure that Nate doesn't get close."

Nate Miller had good reason to hate Jesse. It had been his skill at tracking and his insight that had led them to find Nicole and recover most of the ransom money.

"I'm not going home," Dylan said.

"Fine." Jesse exchanged a glance with Burke, then maneuvered his horse around.

Dylan was flanked by a federal agent on one side and a professional bodyguard on the other. Plus, he was wearing a bulletproof vest. "Good thing I'm not claustrophobic," he said.

"This is how it's going to be until we get you to safety." Jesse drew his rifle and held it at the ready.

Dylan raised an eyebrow. "Are you any good with that?"

"I'm a former marine, a sharpshooter. Is that good enough for you?"

One of the escaped steers plodded toward them. A big, broad Angus—fifteen hundred pounds of premium, grass-fed beef on the hoof—stood in the middle of the road and glared at the men on horseback. He lifted his head and mooed.

"I think he wants us to move," Burke said. "Moo-oo-oove."

"You've been hanging around my sister too much," Dylan said. "Cattle don't talk."

In the distance, he saw the headlights of an approaching vehicle. Whoever it was would have to be patient or take a different route.

When a second steer joined the first, Dylan's horse, Orbison, shifted his weight. In his younger days, Orbison had competed in rodeos as a cutting horse. When he saw cattle running free, the horse's instinct was to get them organized.

But there wasn't much herding Dylan could do with these two men protecting him as though he was made of glass. And, to tell the truth, the other four ranch hands seemed to be doing a good job of moving the herd back into the field. "Might as well head back," he grumbled.

As he wheeled around on Orbison, he heard the sharp crack of a rifle.

## Chapter Five

In the kitchen, Nicole sat at the table with Carolyn and Andrea. They'd convinced her to eat a piece of toast, and they all had mugs of steaming chamomile tea before them.

"How did Dylan take it?" Nicole asked. "While I was kidnapped

"He was a complete wreck," Carolyn said. "That first night, he and his men went riding all over the country-side looking for you, riling up the neighbors. When he got back here, he refused to go to bed even though he was asleep on his feet."

"Stubborn," Nicole said. "That's my husband."

"It was more than that." Carolyn looked down into her tea. "I haven't seen my brother cry since he was ten years old, and we had to put down one of his best horses. During the past few days, I've seen tears."

At least he loved her as much as a favorite horse. She thought of their five years together. A tear had slipped down his cheek when he'd spoken his wedding vows. As it had the first time she'd told him that she loved him. Touching moments.

But he never showed emotion when he was hurt.

That was when he clamped his jaw tight and turned as hard as granite. "I knew this would be rough on him."

Carolyn reached over and touched her arm. "It's good for my brother to express his emotions for a change. Most of the time, he's so bottled up that I think his head is going to explode."

Andrea sighed. "His father was the same way."

"That's for damn sure," Carolyn said. "Daddy used to tell me that only babies cried. And I distinctly recall something about how I shouldn't act like a girl. If he could see my totally feminine condo in Denver, if he knew how much I pay for manicures and pedicures, he'd go through the roof."

"To be fair," Andrea said, "your father and I were part of a different generation. Men are more sensitive now."

Nicole shook her head. "Not Dylan."

Though her son was routinely dismissive toward her, Andrea leapt to his defense. "For the past few days, he's worn his heart on his sleeve."

"His heart?" Carolyn scoffed. "He's been snarling and snapping at everyone."

"Anger is how he covers his emotions," Andrea said. "His fear, his sadness and pain."

Nicole was extremely familiar with Dylan in his cranky mood. She thought back to their argument before she'd gone racing out of the house and into the arms of the kidnappers. She'd been angry, too. Maybe even more than her husband. "Did he mention what we were fighting about before I left the house?"

"He told Burke," Carolyn said.

Why on earth would Dylan confide such a personal matter to someone he barely knew? "Was Burke interrogating him?"

"Nope. Dylan just blurted it out. He must have felt guilty."

*As well he should. He'd been horrible to her.* "It felt like he was choosing the ranch instead of me and the family we might have someday."

"You're trying to get pregnant," Andrea said.

"For almost eight months. I expected to have problems. Being a vet, I've been kicked in the belly a couple of times. But the fertility doc said those injuries weren't entirely the issue. We had a lot of little problems. Low sperm motility. A blocked Fallopian tube. Anyway, it just wasn't happening."

"Did you get Dylan to wear boxer shorts?" Andrea asked.

"As a matter of fact, I did." Black, silky boxer shorts. They had turned out to be as much of a treat for her as for Dylan. "They looked real cute."

Carolyn snorted. "Did he take off his cowboy boots?"

"Sometimes."

Nicole and Dylan had always been sexually compatible, even adventurous. She'd never forget the time he strode into their bedroom wearing his leather chaps and nothing else. Though she was tempted to dwell on that outrageous, sexy image, the conversation drew her back to the subject of children.

"I'd like to be a grandma," Andrea said.

Carolyn beamed. "And I could be the baby's cool aunt in the city. Like Auntie Mame."

Nicole sipped her tea. She still wasn't sure that Dylan really, truly wanted a baby. Though he claimed to be ready for children, there was a definite lack of enthusiasm. It seemed as though he was agreeing because it was easier than fighting with her. And he hated sharing their intimate issues with the doctors at the fertility clinic.

"When the baby is born," Andrea said, "you'll bring him or her to Manhattan, won't you?"

"Only if you arrange for your daughter to visit us at the ranch."

"She'll love it here." Andrea smiled warmly. "Any preteen girl from New York would go crazy for all these handsome cowboys. When I came out west, I certainly did."

And she'd married Sterling Carlisle. "I never knew Dylan's father. Dylan's a lot like him, isn't he?"

"In many ways. They're both strong-willed. Responsible. Deeply loyal."

"Pig-headed," Carolyn said. "And demanding."

Nicole didn't want to see history repeating itself. Andrea and Sterling got divorced; what if her marriage was doomed?

"There is a difference," Andrea said. "Sterling and I never really stood a chance. In spite of how much we loved each other, we didn't want the same things from life. It's not that way with you and Dylan. From the moment I saw you together on your wedding day, I knew you'd make it."

"Why?"

"You have something special. You're both westerners right down to your roots. You're a vet, Nicole. You love animals. And Dylan is a rancher."

"She's right," Carolyn said. "You two have everything in common."

Except for a desire to have children?

She needed to go back to the beginning of their relationship, to remember all those things that had attracted her to Dylan in the first place. To find the man she'd fallen in love with five years ago.

AT THE SOUND of gunfire, Dylan ducked and leaned forward in the saddle—a gut reaction to threat. His next instinct was to search. He squinted through the moonlight. On the side of the road to his left were rocks and shrubs that could be used for cover. The shot had sounded like it had come from farther away, however.

On the horse beside him, Burke dug into his saddlebag and pulled out a pair of night-vision goggles that he fastened onto his head.

"What do you see?" Dylan asked.

"Cows. That truck that was coming down the road turned around."

Even Jesse—a professional bodyguard who had successfully thwarted a number of assassination attempts—was puzzled by the gunshot. He swung his horse around, facing north on the road.

The cattle bawled and stomped their hooves.

The ranch hands on horseback yelled to each other. Every man had a gun in hand.

There was a second shot. And a third.

"That way," Jesse yelled. "He's in that truck."

Jesse quickly dismounted, planted his boots on the pavement near the shoulder of the road and aimed his rifle. Rapid-fire, he got off four shots.

Dylan saw the red flash of brake lights. He couldn't hear the truck's engine with all the noise surrounding him, but he knew the vehicle was driving away. *Nate Miller was getting away.*

It wasn't prudent to chase after that truck; Burke had warned him about being lured into danger. But there was no way in hell that Dylan could sit back and allow that son of a bitch to escape. He dug his heels into Orbison's flanks and took off like a horse-powered rocket.

The dim moonlight reflected off the roof of the truck. He was driving without headlights on the two-lane road.

Dylan raced behind him, riding hard and fast. His horse's hooves pounded the pavement. He wanted to believe that he was closing the gap with every stride, but the fastest horse on the planet couldn't outrun a truck.

Half a mile ahead was the turn leading toward the ranch. With several men standing guard, the people in the house were safe. Nicole was safe. But Dylan hated to think of Nate getting within a mile of her.

If the road had been straight, he would have continued at a gallop. But the truck took a sharp turn and disappeared behind a stand of pine trees.

*The perfect spot for an ambush.* And Dylan was no fool. He directed his horse onto the shoulder of the road, slowing his pace to ride across the unfenced property.

Burke came up beside him. He wasted no time with discussion. With hand signals, he indicated that he'd ride around to the other side of the trees.

If Nate had parked in the cover of those trees, they'd have him surrounded.

Rifle in hand, Jesse rode up beside Dylan. "When we're close," he said, "we approach on foot."

Dylan understood his thinking. He wanted both feet planted on the ground before taking aim. There might only be time for one shot, and he didn't want to miss. Beside a shrub, barren of leaves, he and Jesse dismounted. Dylan drew his handgun.

Together, they picked their way through trees and

shrubs. The dry soil, littered with pinecones and dead leaves, crunched underfoot.

They could see the road. The truck sat there, idling. The old engine rattled. The stink of exhaust tainted the air.

He couldn't see anyone inside. Nate might have left his vehicle, might be on foot, hiding behind a tree trunk or crouched in the shadow of a rock. He didn't expect Nate to play fair.

"Split up," he whispered to Jesse. "I'll go left."

"I'm sticking with you."

They'd have a better chance of finding Nate if they spread out, but there wasn't time for a discussion of strategy. He moved forward.

The truck lights flashed on.

Jesse dropped to one knee and pulled Dylan down beside him. Before either of them could take aim, the truck raced away.

Dylan started toward the pavement, but Jesse held him back. "Stay down."

"He's getting away."

"That's what we should do. Get the hell out of here."

On the opposite side of the road, Burke waved. He was also on foot. "Stay down. I called Jesse's men at the ranch house for back-up."

Dylan crouched beside a waist-high boulder. He had to agree that this set-up didn't feel right. The truck had waited for them to get close. They'd been drawn into this area. It was a trap.

"Damn, Jesse. I want to go after him."

"There could be somebody else driving that truck," Jesse said.

"What? Who?"

"Nate pulled over a hundred thousand bucks off the top of the ransom. He's got money to pay an accomplice."

If Nate was working with someone else, he could have gotten out of the truck. He could be right close by. And they'd be easy targets if they ran to their horses and mounted up.

The brake lights on the truck flashed. The driver stopped and started, driving slowly. Teasing them.

Dylan's handgun wasn't accurate enough for distance shooting. "Take the shot, Jesse. Put holes in his tires."

"Patience."

All this restraint was driving him crazy. Every muscle in his body tensed. He wanted to go after the bastard.

At a bend in the road, the truck stopped. A harsh voice yelled, "Dylan. I know it's you."

He recognized the voice. "That's Nate."

"Are you scared, Dylan? Afraid of me?"

"Come back here," Dylan roared. "Face me like a man."

"You're the coward. You and all your hired body-guards. Hell, your wife is tougher than you are. She didn't cry. Not much, anyway."

The thought of Nicole in the bastard's grasp was too damn much for Dylan to take. He bolted to his feet. He had to go after Nate.

"Wait," Jesse said. "Don't let him get to you. He's trying to draw you out."

Caution be damned. Dylan refused to hide. He had to take action. He strode through the trees with his right arm extended, firing his weapon.

Jesse tackled him, knocked him to the ground.

"Get off me." Dylan's fury gave him strength. He shoved the bodyguard away from him.

Before he could stand up, the night exploded. The air

split in a thunderous roar. A ball of fire burst at the edge of the road.

Dynamite. TNT on a long fuse.

Red and orange flames licked at the surrounding forest. A shower of rocks and dirt rained down upon them.

From far away, Dylan heard Nate Miller laughing.

## Chapter Six

As Nicole sat at the kitchen table, chatting with Carolyn and her mother, a warm sense of drowsiness wrapped around her like a down comforter. They gossiped and talked about homey topics: baking Christmas cookies, shopping for presents, getting started on the decorations for the ranch house.

Christmas had always been Nicole's favorite time of year. She loved making wreaths and tromping through the forest to find the perfect-shaped tree. She hoped there would be a blanket of pure-white snow for Christmas morning.

Eyelids drooping, she gazed down at her hands folded in her lap. The black-and-blue marks circling her wrists reminded her of the kidnapping, and she tugged down her sleeves to cover the bruises. It was better to focus on how good it was to be home, to put those terrible memories out of her mind.

Tomorrow would be a brand-new day. She'd wake up in her warm bed beside her husband—a man with whom she had a great deal in common. For breakfast, there would be bacon and eggs and coffee and...

The hint of a distant explosion shook her out of her

reverie. She bounded to her feet. Her chair fell backward and hit the kitchen floor. "What was that?"

"Trouble," Carolyn said as she whipped out her cell phone. "I'll call Burke."

A shiver shuddered down Nicole's spine. Dylan was out there. Even though she'd begged him to stay with her, to leave the rounding-up of cattle to the others, he'd insisted on riding into danger.

Andrea came up beside her. "Are you all right?"

"Fine."

How quickly her sense of well-being had disappeared! Would she ever feel safe again? Nervously, she picked up her chair and pushed it under the table. Her fingers trembled as she carried her cup to the sink and rinsed the dregs of chamomile tea. If anything had happened to Dylan, she couldn't bear it.

"It's okay," Carolyn announced, waving her cell phone. "Nobody was hurt."

"Thank God," Andrea said. "What made the noise?"

Carolyn pursed her lips. She seemed reluctant to speak. "I don't want either of you to freak out."

"Too late," Nicole said. "What was it?"

"According to Burke, it was…dynamite."

Nicole's knees went weak. Dynamite? She braced herself against the counter.

Carolyn continued, "Nate lured them into an ambush and set off a couple of sticks. But nobody was injured."

"You're sure?" Nicole asked.

"Dylan's fine. He and Jesse and Burke are on their way back. They should be here in a couple of minutes."

In spite of Carolyn's reassurances, images of blood and gore raced through her mind. Dylan never should have gone out there. Why hadn't he listened to her?

The wall phone beside the cupboards rang, and she automatically reached for it. She heard breathing, then a thin, cruel whisper. "I should have left you to die."

The sound of Nate's voice stunned her. She gasped.

"Is anyone with you?" he demanded.

"Y-yes."

"Don't let them know it's me," he whispered. "Give them a smile. Do it, Nicole."

She forced a smile for Carolyn and Andrea, then turned away so they wouldn't see the panic in her eyes.

"I'm still in charge, Nicole. Don't doubt it. Not for a minute."

She wasn't his hostage, anymore. He couldn't force her to do his bidding. "I'm not going to—"

"Silence," he hissed. "I almost killed Dylan tonight. He's a hothead, isn't he? Isn't he?"

"Yes." She had to admit the truth. Dylan knew better than to leave the house, but he'd put himself directly in the line of fire.

"Your big, brave husband doesn't take very good care of himself. He takes risks."

Oh, God. Nate was right. Dylan didn't know how to be a coward, didn't know when to back down.

"Doesn't he?"

"Yes."

"I'm a patient man, Nicole. I've waited this long for my revenge. I can wait a little longer. Until I see Dylan riding by himself within the range of my rifle. Or maybe I'll use a car bomb. I'm handy with a knife."

"What do you want?"

"Do exactly as I say, or Dylan dies."

"I understand."

"Write down my phone number."

There was a message pad attached to the wall and a pencil on a string. She didn't want to follow his orders. But if she didn't do as he said, if she failed to make him happy, the consequences would be terrible. She scribbled down the number as he recited it, then she repeated it back to him.

"Very good," he said. "Get yourself a cell phone, Nicole. Call me at that number."

"Of course."

"If you tell anyone you've spoken to me, you know what will happen." There was no inflection in his whispering. The lack of emotion terrified her as he continued, "I'll destroy everything and everyone you care about. I won't stop."

"Yes," she said. "I know."

"Good night, Nicole. Dream of me."

When she replaced the receiver on the hook, her hand was surprisingly steady. After seven days in captivity, she was more accustomed to prisoner behavior than to the uncertainty of real life. She tucked the scrap of paper with his phone number into the pocket of her robe. She had to appease Nate Miller. To keep her family safe.

"Who was that?" Carolyn asked.

"One of the neighbors. The explosion woke her." The falsehood slid easily through her lips. She had to lie. There was no choice. "What else did Burke tell you?"

"Nate got away."

"Of course he did."

Nate was clever and cruel—more dangerous than any of them knew. They underestimated him, didn't comprehend the depth of his hatred for the Carlisle family.

"Something's wrong," Carolyn said as she came closer. "What is it?"

"I'm tired. I should lie down."

"Of course," Andrea said. "Come with me, dear. I'll help you up to bed."

Dylan's mother meant to be kind, but Nicole felt like snapping at her. She bit her lip to keep from saying something she'd regret. *No one can know. I have to stay in control.* Stiffly, she climbed the staircase with Andrea at her side. At the door to her room, Nicole turned to the sophisticated woman from New York. "I'm fine now."

"If there's anything I can do—"

"Thank you," she said curtly. "Good night, Andrea."

Nicole closed the door, shutting out further offers of help and kindness. No one could understand what she'd been through. Not Andrea. Not Carolyn. And especially not Dylan.

He'd never get it. He was too busy being tough and macho to pay attention to her needs.

She took off her robe and hung it on a peg in the closet, leaving the note with Nate Miller's phone number in the pocket. There was no way to escape him. She'd tried. For seven days she'd tried, but he was obsessed. Just as Burke said. Obsessive. All he wanted was to destroy her family.

She slipped between the covers on her bed and leaned her back against the pillows. If she had to sacrifice herself to save Dylan, she'd do it. No matter how much he ticked her off, she still cared about him. At her core, at the center of her being, she couldn't imagine what her life would be like without him. But could she still love him if he denied her the family she wanted so desperately?

From downstairs, she heard the men arrive. They were loud and boisterous, and their boots clomped in the entryway. She heard laughter and imagined Carolyn throwing her arms around her big, handsome FBI agent.

Without knocking, Dylan opened the bedroom door. His face was smudged with dirt. His green eyes blazed as he crossed the room and sat on the edge of the bed.

"You were right," he said.

She gasped with relief. Those were the best words he could have spoken. "Say it again."

"You. Were. Right."

She scooted across the bed and wrapped her arms tightly around him. "Thank God, you understand now. If anything had happened to you, I…"

"Nothing happened." He lifted her onto his lap and held her close against his chest. "We're safe. Both of us."

She hardly dared to believe it was true, but he was here, safely in her arms. She tilted her head up and kissed him. Familiar sensations swirled through her. In the five years they'd been together, there had been thousands of kisses. Maybe even millions. But the firm pressure of his mouth against hers never failed to arouse her. His teeth tugged at her lower lip, and she kissed him harder. His taste was sweet nectar.

Nestling into his embrace, she marveled at how perfectly they fitted together. He knew the secrets of her body, knew how she liked to be held, knew that she would shiver with pleasure when he caressed her back with feathery strokes.

He was her man. Her lover. Her husband.

His lips brushed the line of her cheekbone. He nipped at her earlobe. "I'll always take care of you," he said. "I won't let Nate come near you. Not ever again."

"He wants to kill you, Dylan."

"I'm not afraid."

She pulled away from him. "You should be."

"He won't hurt me. Nate's a coward and a fool."

She shoved at her husband's chest. "Nate wasn't so foolish when he was holding me captive. He outsmarted you, the sheriff and the FBI. I'd call that pretty damned clever."

"Forget about him."

Dylan leaned closer for another kiss, but she wasn't about to be seduced into complacency. Her vigilance would keep them alive. She climbed off his lap and stood before him. "I can't forget."

He held out a hand toward her. "I didn't mean to—"

She slapped his hand away. "He almost killed you tonight because you didn't listen to me. I warned you not to go out there."

"I already said you were right."

She wanted more than an apology. She needed his full assurance that he wouldn't take any more risks. "When you heard that the fence had been cut, you should have known it was a trap. And it wasn't necessary for you to respond. We have over thirty employees."

"Not all of them are at the ranch," he said. "There are a couple of guys out in the far grazing pastures. And some had to stay here, guarding the house."

"You know what I mean." She refused to be sidetracked by numbers. "Lucas could handle the situation. You should have left the wrangling to him and his men."

A shadow darkened the pale green of his eyes. He was hiding something.

"What is it?" she demanded.

"Lucas is dead." He looked down at his boots.

Shocked, she stepped backward. The back of her legs hit the chair by the window, and she abruptly sat. Lucas Mann had been the foreman at the Carlisle ranch for as long as she'd been here. The bowlegged old cowboy with a plug of tobacco in his cheek was an integral part of this place. "What happened?"

"He betrayed us," Dylan said. "Lucas was working with the Sons of Freedom when they first started their sabotage. He took payoffs. And he stood in the way of our investigation."

She didn't care. Lucas had been part of their family. At Thanksgiving, he'd sat across the table from her, wearing a freshly ironed shirt, with his thinning hair neatly combed. She couldn't believe he was dead. "How was he killed?"

"When Carolyn was delivering the ransom, he tried to help her. He was shot."

*Nate killed him.*

Her worst fears were coming true. Nate had promised to destroy the people she loved, and he'd already started with Lucas. "Have you spoken to his family?"

"He had no one," Dylan said.

"Except for us. We need to make the funeral arrangements," she said. "I'm assuming there was an autopsy. Has his body been released?"

"Didn't you hear me? Lucas turned against us."

"So what? He made a mistake."

"He lied to me. He willfully destroyed our property."

"He was part of our family." Lucas had given years of his life to the Carlisle ranch, and his contribution should be recognized. He died trying to protect Carolyn. "You have to forgive him."

"The hell I do."

She shook her head in disbelief. What had happened to the kind, sensitive man she'd married five years ago? When had he turned so judgmental? All that mattered to Dylan was his precious ranch. Lucas had destroyed his property and couldn't be forgiven for that sin. "You'd carry a grudge beyond the grave?"

"Some treachery can't be forgiven." He stood before her—tall and undeniably strong. "I thought I'd lost you, that I'd never see you again. And Lucas was working against me. Against us."

"You used to be forgiving. Remember that time when you caught that teenager poaching on our land? You could have turned him in to the sheriff, but you didn't. His family was going through a hard time, and you gave him a job."

Dylan frowned at the memory. "That was a long time ago."

"I don't know you anymore. All you think about is business. You used to take days off, and we'd go for a long rides. You used to bring me wildflower bouquets."

"Is that what you want?"

"I want the man I married. A kind man. A good man." She sank into the chair, too tired to fight. "Please leave, Dylan."

DYLAN WINCED. Her words were a knife in his heart. His wife was ordering him to leave, telling him to get the hell out of their bedroom. It wasn't the first time that one of their arguments had ended with him sleeping on the sofa in his office.

But that wasn't going to happen tonight. He couldn't be angry at her. Not after what she'd been through.

"You shouldn't be alone," he said.

"I'll be fine."

She rose from the chair. Her long cotton nightgown reached almost to the floor. Though her shoulders were back and her posture erect, she seemed wobbly. Her feet were bare, and her pink toes looked tiny and vulnerable.

He wanted to go to her, to support her. But he held back.

"You've been through an ordeal," he said. "I shouldn't have left you sleeping alone before, and I won't make that mistake again."

She moved toward the bed, sat on the edge. Her blue eyes appeared huge in her thin face. "I'm tired."

"You can lie down." He settled in the overstuffed chair she had vacated. "Get some sleep. I'll be right here if you need anything."

He reached toward the bedside lamp to turn it off, but she stopped him. "I'd rather leave the light on."

"Whatever you want."

She looked toward him. For a moment, he thought she might invite him into the bed with her. Instead, she slipped under the covers and closed her eyes.

He pulled off his boots and tried to find a comfortable position. Not that he expected to get much sleep tonight. Nicole had given him a lot to think about.

She'd been right when she'd said he wasn't the same man she'd married. Five years ago, he'd been struggling to manage the ranching operations after his dad passed away. Dylan knew his responsibilities. His father had lectured him daily.

In the years before his death, Sterling Carlisle had been a hard-driving teacher who didn't make allowances for failure. He'd been an innovator. His changes—using free-range organic processes to raise an antibiotic-free, grass-fed herd—had revolutionized the industry in Colorado.

Dylan had inherited a big job. Though he was only twenty-seven at the time, he needed had to prove himself. When it came to the ranch, he couldn't afford to be a dumb kid. Even small mistakes could cost a fortune.

Lucas Mann had helped with practical advice and guidance. He never hesitated to speak up when he didn't agree. They'd butted heads. They'd made amends. And Dylan missed that old cowboy. He'd shed some tears when he heard that Lucas was dead.

He looked toward the bed where Nicole was breathing slowly and steadily. The glow from the bedside lamp highlighted her delicate features. She was right about Lucas. They needed to bury the old man and pay him respect.

*In spite of his betrayal?* Dylan didn't want to send the message that he accepted traitors. There had to be consequences for bad behavior. Life wasn't all daisy chains and sunsets. There were hard decisions to be made.

Those thoughts echoed inside his head. *There are consequences. Make the hard decisions. Plan for the best but be prepared for the worst.*

Leaning back in the chair, he groaned. When had he become such a stubborn cuss? When had he turned into his father?

## Chapter Seven

The next morning, Dylan tried to get back into his normal routine. After making sure Nicole was okay, he showered, dressed, went downstairs, got coffee and went to his office. His intention was to dig into the stack of unopened mail and deal with an e-mail in-box that was stuffed like a Christmas turkey.

For a full week, the running of the ranch had been on autopilot. Now, there was work to be done. Invoices to be signed. Schedules to be reassigned.

*Back to normal.* That was what he wanted.

His instinct to stay through the night with Nicole—in spite of her objection—had been a good one. She'd wakened twice.

The first time, she'd been breathing hard, gasping. Both her hands drew into fists that she held to her mouth. When he came near the bed, she'd slapped at him. In a hard voice, she'd told him to get away from her and had let loose a string of graphic profanity—words he'd never heard from his sweet, gentle wife. Dylan had known better than to take her insults personally; she wasn't talking to him but fighting off the demons that haunted her sleep.

Instead of waking her or touching her, he'd sat beside the bed and spoken softly, telling her that she was safe. She was home. Everything was going to be all right. Gradually, she'd slipped back into peaceful sleep.

The second time she woke up, she'd been sobbing. Again, he'd reassured her.

Though he told himself that she'd be all right, he figured that he'd better take Carolyn's advice and call in a doctor. Maybe Nicole needed a sleeping pill, a sedative, something for her nerves.

*She'll be all right. She has to be.* It might take a while, but he had to believe that Nicole would forget about her ordeal and remember that she was his wife, that they had a good life together.

Dylan got down to business. He tore open a manila envelope from the local law firm he used for day-to-day operations. The first line of the cover letter read, "Regarding the death of Lucas Mann..."

The words stung. He dropped the attorney's papers on his desk. *Who the hell am I kidding?* Life at the Carlisle ranch would never be the way it was before. He couldn't turn back the clock, couldn't bring Lucas back to life, couldn't erase Nicole's heartache and make her love him the way she had before. Whether he liked it or not, things had changed.

Pushing his paperwork out of the way, he folded his arms on the desktop, leaned forward and rested his head. Tears pooled behind his eyelids, but he wouldn't cry. Not while he was sitting at the desk that had once belonged to his father.

He closed his eyes. *I'm tired.* He'd gotten only a few winks of sleep last night. *So tired.*

When he opened his eyes and looked at his watch, he

saw that two hours had passed. It was after nine o'clock, and the whole household was awake. He heard voices and laughter and the sounds of people walking around. Outside the door to his office, life was happening.

On a normal day, he'd stay right here and work. He was tempted to ignore his responsibilities and join the rest of the family. *Things had changed.*

Just maybe, change was good.

Before the kidnapping, his relationship with Nicole had been rocky. They'd grown apart. He'd tried his best…

Dylan stopped that thought. He took a sip of his ice-cold coffee and faced the truth. He'd taken Nicole for granted. He hadn't paid enough attention to her. And now, if he didn't watch out, he'd lose her for sure.

He cleared his desktop, making room for a new set of priorities. And he put his wife at the top of the list.

A COUPLE OF HOURS LATER, Dylan was back to his office, savoring a fresh cup of coffee. He'd made definite progress on Project Make Nicole Happy and he couldn't wait for her to see the results. The world felt a whole lot brighter as he rose from his swivel chair and went to the window.

The snowfall had started. Forecasters predicted a two- to three-inch dusting for today and more tomorrow. He was glad. They needed the moisture in the pastures.

A black SUV with the Delta County Sheriff's Department logo on the side came up the drive and parked in front of the house. Dylan went to the front door to meet Sheriff Trainer. Though Carolyn and Burke would probably want in on this conversation, he preferred a one-on-one talk. Whenever his sister was involved, things got complicated.

Dylan directed the sheriff to his office, closed the door and returned to his seat behind the desk. "Coffee?"

"I've already had three cups."

And a half a pack of cigarettes from the smell of him. After he dropped his uniform jacket and hat on the sofa, Trainer settled into one of the leather chairs on the other side of the desk. The lines etched into his long, lean face had deepened during the course of this investigation. He looked years older.

"Let me guess," Dylan said. "You've got good news and bad news."

"That's about the size of it."

The sheriff and his deputies had done a competent job in processing evidence and working on the crime scenes, but their investigative work in solving Nicole's kidnapping had been less than impressive. Burke and the FBI had taken care of the Sons of Freedom smuggling operation. Jesse Longbridge had uncovered the clues that pointed to Nate Miller.

"Start with the good," Dylan said.

"We found the truck Nate was driving."

"Using the license-plate number Jesse gave you?"

"That's right." The sheriff scowled. He didn't much like Jesse, especially since Jesse and Fiona Grant were together now. For a while, the sheriff had considered Fiona a suspect. "It was abandoned on a back road in Delta. The truck was reported stolen last night."

"Did you talk to the owner?"

"I did, and I don't think he's guilty of anything other than stupidity. He was in a tavern, drinking, and left his car keys on the table. It's just as well. He wasn't in any condition to drive."

Nate had stolen the truck, then abandoned it. "Do you have any idea what Nate's driving now?"

"I already impounded all the vehicles at the Circle

M that belonged to the SOF. But Nate's truck doesn't seem to be anywhere around here."

"So, he's driving his own truck. Right?"

"I guess." The sheriff scowled.

The lackadaisical attitude was beginning to tick Dylan off. "Have you got your men out looking for him? You could set up roadblocks."

"Not going to happen," the sheriff said. "During the past week, my deputies have put in six months' worth of overtime. I can't authorize more."

"Why the hell not?"

"The county has a budget."

"Not my problem," Dylan said. "Last night, Nate Miller set off a couple of sticks of dynamite trying to kill me. That kind of criminal act deserves your full attention."

"I'm doing what I can." The sheriff fidgeted. "There's no point in running in circles. Nate's good at covering his tracks. It's not likely we'll find him sitting at the café in Riverton, munching on a jelly donut."

Locating Nate wouldn't be easy. Dylan understood that, but his level of frustration was nearing the boiling point. With Nate Miller at large, he and his family were in danger. Every time they left the house, they were targets. He didn't like being trapped. "What steps *are* you taking?"

The sheriff licked his lips, probably yearning for another smoke. "Waiting for leads."

Determined to control his temper, Dylan rose slowly to his feet. "Let me get this straight, Sheriff. Your basic plan is to do nothing."

"I'll tell you one thing I've been doing ever since this mess got started. I've been holding off the media. It wasn't hard to sidestep our local people, but the Denver news stations have been snooping around."

He knew that Carolyn's publicity and promotion department in Denver had been working to keep things quiet. The last thing he wanted was a bunch of reporters shining a spotlight on Nicole's kidnapping—that was sure to lead to a focus on their marital problems, including their visits to the fertility clinic. And wouldn't that be a special piece of hell? "Please tell me you haven't spoken to anyone."

"Not yet. But they want me to hold a press conference and go on TV. One of those national tabloids called."

Dylan planted his palms on the desktop and leaned across to confront the sheriff directly. "All of a sudden, doing nothing sounds like a mighty fine idea."

"I've got some advice for you. Those reporters are persistent. Sooner or later, they'll snag an interview with somebody. If you and Nicole want to avoid that spotlight, you should leave town."

And let Nate Miller chase him off his own property? This was his home. He'd do whatever necessary to defend it.

The door to his office swung open, and Nicole stepped inside. She looked pretty this morning, dressed in jeans and a blue turtleneck under a matching button-up shirt. Her blond hair was neatly brushed and tucked behind her ears. Her eyes were bright.

She went directly to the sheriff and shook his hand. "I want to thank you for all your help."

"Just doing my job. You're looking well."

"That I am." Her determined smile almost covered up the underlying fear Dylan had seen last night as she continued, "I'd like to know when you can release Lucas Mann's body for burial."

"Within the next few days." The sheriff stood and hitched up his belt, getting ready to leave. "I was contacted by the attorney who filed Lucas's will."

"Steve Stanley in Delta," Dylan said.

"That's the guy," the sheriff said.

"His firm handles the basic paperwork for all our employees." Full-timers at the ranch were required to fill out a will to go along with their health- and life-insurance policies. "I got the paperwork from Steve informing us that there wasn't any next of kin. Lucas's beneficiary was the homeless shelter in Delta."

Nicole glanced at him. "The same place where you donate a side of beef every quarter?"

He nodded. He should have remembered that shelter last night when she was accusing him of being insensitive. He'd made a lot of charitable contributions. Being in the beef business, he hated to see anyone go hungry.

"In Lucas's will," the sheriff said, "he specifically asked to be cremated. He didn't specify what should happen to the ashes."

"If there's no legal problem," Nicole said, "I'd like to have his remains."

The sheriff patted her shoulder. In seconds, his demeanor had switched from cold and hostile to genuine warmth. "You're a good woman, Nicole. I'm sure that Lucas—wherever he is—would be glad that you were taking care of him."

"He was family," she said. "We loved him."

"I know you did."

If this conversation got much sweeter, Dylan thought he might go into insulin shock. He circled his desk and held open the office door. "Okay, Sheriff. Thanks for stopping by."

"No need to rush," Nicole said. "Would you like coffee? Polly made some of her famous raisin rolls."

From down the hall, Dylan heard the front doorbell. Carolyn answered, and called out, "Nicole! Come here, Nicole."

This wasn't happening the way Dylan had planned. He'd hoped to be alone with his wife when the surprise arrived. He'd wanted her to be looking only at him.

No such luck.

Standing in the front foyer were two deliverymen from a flower shop in Delta. Each of them held two dozen red roses in vases. "These are for Nicole Carlisle," one of the men announced. "From her adoring husband."

Instead of cooing with delight, her eyes narrowed as she looked from the bouquets to him and back again. She didn't appear to be pleased. *What the hell?* She had to be happy. What woman wouldn't be thrilled by four dozen red roses?

He stepped toward her. "You said you wanted posies."

"Thank you."

The perfunctory statement of gratitude fell from her lips and landed on the floor with a thud. What had he done wrong this time?

# Chapter Eight

After bidding the sheriff goodbye, Nicole directed the deliverymen to place the roses on the table in the dining room. A massive display, the flowers were absolutely gorgeous with their long stems, green leaves and sprigs of baby's breath.

In the early years of their marriage, Dylan had often surprised Nicole with a bouquet of wildflowers he'd picked along the trail. The spontaneous gesture had delighted her. It had showed that he was thinking of her. He'd taken the trouble to dismount and gather brightly colored posies.

Roses from the florist weren't the same. Anybody could pick up a phone and make a call.

With a sigh, she plucked one long-stemmed rose from the vase. This rich crimson would fit nicely into her plans for Christmas decorations, though she doubted her husband had considered the color from a decorating standpoint.

He stood close behind her. "Do you like them?"

"Of course." He was trying, and she had to give him points for the effort. "Really, Dylan. They're lovely."

"Well," Carolyn said as she came close and inhaled the somewhat overwhelming fragrance. "If you ask me—"

"Nobody asked," her brother said. "Nobody ever asks, but it never stops you from talking."

Ignoring Dylan, she continued, "I like the roses better than poinsettias. We'll tie some green ribbons around the vases, and they'll be perfect."

"I want to get started decorating today," Nicole said as she trailed the velvety rose petal along her cheek. "It's only two weeks until Christmas. I'm kind of surprised that nothing's been done."

"Blame your husband," Carolyn said. "Andrea and I were ready to deck the halls, but Dylan said no."

Puzzled, Nicole asked, "Why wouldn't you let them decorate?"

"Because that's your job," he said. "I know how much you love Christmas. There's a story behind every ornament you hang on the tree. I told Carolyn we had to wait for you."

"Really?" She remembered their meeting in the forest when she'd been forced at gunpoint to tell him she wanted a divorce. "How did you know I'd come back?"

The green in his corduroy shirt emphasized the color of his eyes. A deep red flushed his cheeks. "I knew you'd be home for Christmas."

His trust touched her heart. No matter what she'd told him, he believed in her. *In their relationship.* She held out her hand. "The holidays have always been a special time."

When his fingers laced through hers, she felt the old Dylan returning—the bashful cowboy who blushed and wasn't afraid to show he cared. This was the man she'd fallen in love with.

"We've got things to do," Carolyn said. "Fiona and her daughter are coming over this afternoon with Jesse to help with the decorating. I'll find Burke, and we'll bring down the Christmas boxes from the attic."

"And we need a tree," Dylan said.

With the light snow falling, today would have been the perfect time to head out on horseback and search the forests until they spotted the perfect Christmas tree. Not too short or tall. The branches needed to be symmetrical.

She loved that tradition. But not this year. "We can't go roaming through the forests. Not while Nate's lurking around."

"Not to worry," Dylan said. "I have a plan."

Curious, she followed him back to his office. "Another surprise? You've been busy this morning."

"You inspire me, darlin'."

As he sat her in one of the leather chairs facing the desk, his hand lingered on her shoulder. A gentle touch. A sweet reminder. She felt herself being drawn into the familiar pattern of their life together.

Dylan called a number on his cell phone. At the same time, he turned his computer screen around so it was facing her. After a brief consultation on the phone, he tapped a few strokes on the computer keyboard. A shaky picture appeared.

"It's a live feed," Dylan said. "I sent a couple of the ranch hands out to find you the perfect tree."

Though nothing could be as good as their previous tree-chopping adventures, this was a decent substitute. She jumped to her feet and gave her husband a hug. "You're a genius."

"Not really." He gave her a peck on the cheek. "I'm just a thoughtful, sensitive guy with a great big heart."

"And a great big ego to match."

He turned the cell phone to speaker. "Talk to me, MacKenzie."

"Sure thing, boss. This tree's about ten feet tall."

"Have one of the other guys stand next to it so we can compare."

Nicole squinted at the image on the screen. "It's lopsided. And too skinny."

"We'll keep looking," MacKenzie said. "There's a whole forest to choose from."

"Turn the camera around," she said. "I want to see who my Christmas elves are."

"Don't call me an elf, ma'am."

"Of course not." She recognized the other men with MacKenzie. One was Larry. The other had the nickname of Dirty Tom, though she'd never found out why. It was probably best she didn't know. "Thank you, guys. I appreciate this."

"Keep to the south sides of the hills," Dylan said. "Those trees get more sun."

The camera jostled as the cowboys mounted up and rode through the lightly falling snow. After fifteen minutes of directing them, Nicole still hadn't spotted the right tree. But she was enjoying the search.

"This was a great idea, Dylan."

"Just because we're stuck inside the house, it doesn't mean we can't find the best Christmas tree."

He was sitting beside her, looking pleased with himself. A half grin lifted the corner of his mouth. The laugh lines at the corners of his deep-set eyes crinkled.

"When you came down to your office," she said, "I thought you'd be locked inside all day. Taking care of business."

"I've got my priorities straight. My number-one project is titled Make Nicole Happy."

"I'm even more important than the cattle?"

"You're my little lost dogie that strayed. I need to bring you back to the herd."

Being compared to an orphaned calf wasn't exactly a compliment, but she appreciated the thought.

The office door whipped open, and Carolyn strode into the room. "We've got trouble. Take a look out front."

Peering through the window, Nicole saw a news truck with a satellite dish on top. The television news crew had been stopped at the gate by the cowboys guarding the house. Even from this distance, she could see a woman reporter with microphone in hand.

"I'd better get out there," Carolyn said, "before that pretty reporter convinces one of our guys to talk."

"Give them the two-word response," Dylan said. "No comment."

"Thanks for the advice, baby brother, but I know how to handle the media." She tossed her head, and her black ponytail flipped back and forth. "This might be a good opportunity for publicity."

Nicole couldn't imagine anything more humiliating than media attention. She'd barely been able to tell her family the sketchy outline of what she'd endured. Having her story displayed in the media would be devastating. "Please, Carolyn. I don't want my photograph next to the check-out line in the supermarket."

"There's no reason for you to feel bad. You didn't do anything wrong."

"You heard her," Dylan said. "Give them a 'no comment.' That's all."

"If that's the way you want to play it, okay." Carolyn

stalked toward the door. "I won't say one word about the kidnapping. But I'm not passing up the chance to talk about Carlisle Certified Organic Beef. National publicity won't hurt our bottom line."

Nicole returned to the chair facing the computer screen. The live feed showed a very nice lodgepole pine.

"How about this one?" MacKenzie asked.

Following her instructions, he circled the tree and knocked a dusting of snow from the branches. Her gaze was distracted. Though she tried to recapture her former mood of fun and celebration, the bubble had popped.

"The tree is great," she said. "Chop it down."

She heard a shout from Dirty Tom. The camera bobbled.

Dylan snapped, "What's going on?"

"We got company," MacKenzie said.

"Don't take chances," Dylan ordered. "Draw your weapons. Be prepared for an attack."

The camera swung around, giving them a snowy view of what was happening. She saw Dirty Tom aim his rifle. The other man rode downhill. Melting snowflakes smeared the lens.

Over the cell phone she heard more shouting. This could be Nate, moving in for an attack. His threats focused on Dylan, but she wouldn't put it past him to go after other employees at the Carlisle ranch. Nobody was truly safe until he was taken into custody.

Gripping the arms of the chair, she felt her body tense and the blood drain from her face. The only way to stop Nate was to obey him. He'd told her to get a cell phone and call him, but how could she? How could she betray Dylan?

"Tom got the drop on them," MacKenzie said. "It's two guys. What do you want us to do with them?"

"Turn the camera around," Dylan said, "so I can see them."

Through the lens they saw two men in parkas and stocking caps. One of them had a shoulder-mounted camera. The other held a microphone.

"Reporters," Dylan muttered. "Go ahead and shoot them."

Before MacKenzie took the boss at his word, Nicole jumped in. "Escort those gentlemen off our property. Don't talk to them."

"One of them says we can be on TV."

"Listen to me," Dylan said. His voice was harsh. "The first man who talks to the media is fired. Is that clear?"

"But we've got to say something." MacKenzie sounded confused. "How are they going to know what to do unless we—"

"Talk about the weather. You can tell them your life story. Hell, you can whip out a guitar and sing them a song. But don't talk about the kidnapping. Got it?"

"You bet, boss. We'll get rid of these guys and come back for the tree."

The live feed went dead, and Nicole slumped back in the chair. Her heart was beating fast. Though she was free of the chains Nate had used to keep her prisoner, she was still under his control. As long as he threatened, she couldn't forget him or pretend that he didn't exist.

When Dylan touched her shoulder, she flinched.

"Are you okay?" he asked.

"I thought it was Nate. That he was coming after MacKenzie and the other guys."

"They're okay, darlin'. Everything's going to be fine."

*If only I could believe him.*

"Dylan, I need a cell phone."

AFTER LUNCH, the Christmas tree was set up in the living room, the boxes of decorations had been brought down from the attic and Nicole was in the kitchen with Polly Sanchez and Andrea. There were gingerbread cookies in the oven and hot cinnamon punch on the stove.

Trying to absorb the festive spirit, Nicole inhaled. She wanted to see the day through a rosy glow, to enjoy the sounds of laughter and carols playing on the stereo. *Santa Claus is coming to town.* She hummed along. "You'd better watch out." That was ominous. Who knew that Christmas had such dark undercurrents? *Watch out, watch out…*

Her ears pricked up as she heard a familiar voice from the front entryway. Doctor Maud Applegate.

She rushed down the hall and threw her arms around the tall, rosy-cheeked woman in a long, reddish-brown parka that made her look like a giant hot dog topped with a wild mop of curly blond hair. She trusted Doc Maud more than anyone but Dylan. Except, of course, when it came to fashion. Maud could diagnose ten different bovine parasites from a quick glance through a microscope, but she was incapable of putting together an outfit that matched.

Nicole looked up into her friend's bright blue eyes. "I've missed you."

"It's only been a couple of weeks." Maud squeezed her again. "A lot's happened. Oh, Nicole, I'm so sorry."

"I didn't know you were coming. Did Dylan call you?"

"He did. And he wanted a favor." Maud pulled away

from Nicole. "I'd like to introduce Doctor Sarah Lowell. She's going to examine you and make sure you're all right."

Looking over his shoulder, she caught a glimpse of her clever husband. She'd told Dylan a dozen times that she didn't need a doctor, but he knew she couldn't refuse Maud. She politely greeted the attractive young doctor with straight brown hair and long bangs that covered her eyebrows.

Both women shed their coats, and Maud revealed her version of holiday finery—a green paisley jacket, red blouse and a giant Santa Claus belt buckle. There were various other bangles and dangles—earrings, bracelets and necklaces. She looked like a walking Christmas tree.

"I've got to ask," Nicole said. "Where did you get all the jewelry?"

"You know how I do those talks in the grade school about pet safety? This year, the kids brought me gifts. I couldn't decide which I liked best, so I'm wearing them all."

Maud had always loved kids—a love made poignant by the fact that she couldn't have children of her own.

"Shall we get started?" Dr. Lowell asked.

"We'll go upstairs to my bedroom." As they climbed the staircase, Nicole asked, "Are you new in town?"

"I've been here a couple of months. I'm on a reimbursement program that pays off some of my med-school debt if I take a job in a rural area."

"How did you meet Maud?"

"It's the same old story," Maud said. "Girl moves to town, finds a stray cat, brings the kitty to the vet for shots and falls in love with my assistant, Tony."

"Tony's a great guy." Nicole opened the door to her bedroom and escorted the other two women inside. "I'm afraid we've wasted your time in coming here, Sarah. There's really nothing wrong with me."

The young doctor's expression turned serious. "You'd like to believe that you were completely untouched by being held captive for seven days?"

"Untouched?" Nicole frowned. "That wouldn't be the word I'd choose."

"Let's sit over here by the window."

The three women arranged themselves. Sarah took the chair Dylan had slept in last night. Nicole perched on the matching chair beside the table. Maud slipped off her loafers and sat cross-legged on the bed.

It seemed like an odd start to an examination.

Nicole asked, "Should I take my shirt off? Roll up the sleeves?"

"I'd like to ask a few questions first," Sarah said.

"Right." She nodded. "You need to know about prior illnesses and allergies."

The young doctor smiled. "I'm a medical doctor, fully capable of giving you a physical checkup. I work in a clinic with other doctors who have other specialties. My area of expertise is psychiatry."

Nicole sat back in her chair and folded her arms below her breasts. A psychiatrist? "Does Dylan know about this?"

"Lord, no," Maud said. "Introducing you to Sarah was my idea."

Nicole had nothing against mental-health professionals. In her work as a vet, she'd seen how the emotional component played into wellness and behavior, even in a herd of cattle. But she'd always thought of herself as a well-grounded individual—not someone who needed psychiatric counseling.

On the other hand, she'd never been kidnapped and held captive before.

## Chapter Nine

After half an hour's conversation, Nicole's mouth was dry and her palms sweaty. She'd related the chronology of her time in captivity with a few more details than she'd told to the others, including the heart-pounding panic when Nate sealed her mouth with duct tape. When she talked about it, a gag reflex tightened her throat.

She sat back in her chair. "Well, Sarah? What's your diagnosis?"

"It wouldn't be going out on a limb to say that you've been traumatized. Do you agree?"

"Yes." As a vet, Nicole didn't have the luxury of talking to her patients. She couldn't look a bawling steer in the eye and ask where it hurt. The only way to understand was poking and prodding. That sort of guesswork wouldn't be necessary for her own treatment. "How do I get better?"

"You've already taken the first step by acknowledging your trauma. Tell me about your physical symptoms."

"Upset stomach. I've vomited twice. I'm tense and irritable. Having trouble sleeping."

"Falling asleep?"

Nicole thought for a moment, trying to be precise. "I

can nod off, but I'm not getting a good rest. I'm wakeful. Tossing and turning."

"And your dreams?"

"I don't remember." She wasn't ready or willing to reveal the depth of her fear. "Nate Miller is a very creepy guy. He's obsessed with destroying the Carlisle family."

"I want to talk about you."

"He scares me. Him and his threats." She hastened to add, "Last night, Dylan went chasing after him and almost got himself blown to bits. Nate set off dynamite."

Sarah nodded. "I heard about that."

Her easygoing, encouraging manner almost made Nicole forget that she was talking to a shrink. Almost. "Nate Miller is a very dangerous person. He's already killed our foreman, Lucas Mann."

"And you're afraid he'll hurt someone else you love."

"I can't stand to lose anyone else," Nicole said.

"Have you lost others?"

"My parents." The remembered sorrow surrounding the death of her mother and then her father only a year later washed through her in a sudden, unexpected surge. She grabbed a tissue from the box on the table to dab away the tears. "Oh, hell."

"It's all right to miss them," Sarah said.

"Well, yes. But I don't usually start crying when I think of them." Her emotions were in turmoil. She couldn't control herself. "How long will it take me to get over this?"

"I'd like to set up regular appointments," Sarah said. "In the meantime, I'll prescribe anti-anxiety medication."

"No drugs," Nicole said firmly.

Maud sat up straighter on the bed. "Why's that?"

"Just because." Nicole knew she wasn't being a good patient, but she didn't care. She'd talked as much as she intended to. "Sarah, could you run some blood tests for me? I've been feeling weak, maybe anemic. I don't think Nate was drugging me, but I'd like to make sure."

"No problem."

Sarah quickly went through the physical part of the examination and complimented Nicole on her self-treatment of her bruises and abrasions. After drawing a couple of vials of blood, she arranged to come back to the ranch in a few days. "But you can call me—anytime you want to talk."

After Nicole showed Sarah downstairs to the front door and said goodbye, she took Maud by the arm and dragged her down the hallway to Dylan's office. She peeked inside, making sure nobody was there. Then she pulled Maud into the room and closed the door. "Why did you bring a psychiatrist?"

"She's good, isn't she?"

"Answer my question."

Maud straightened the tangle of necklaces around her throat. "When Dylan called, he told me you refused to see a doctor. I trust your judgment enough to believe you. Physically, I think you're going to heal in a few days. But he also mentioned trouble sleeping, tension, nervousness. He's worried about you."

"Dylan wants everything to get back to normal as soon as possible."

"Don't you?" Maud asked.

She wasn't so sure. "To be completely honest, normal wasn't so great. Dylan and I have been arguing. I'm not sure I want things to go back to the way we were before the kidnapping. I want a change."

"Does this have anything to do with the reason you refused to take medication?"

She sat on the long leather sofa. She trusted Maud. They came from the same town in Wyoming, and she had known Maud for most of her life. It was because of Maud that Nicole had moved to this area to work in Maud's veterinary clinic. Still, it was difficult to talk about her fertility troubles with someone who wasn't part of the family. Nicole inhaled a breath and blurted, "I want to have a baby."

"Fan-tabulous!" Maud dove onto the sofa beside her and gave her a hug. "You'll make a terrific mom."

"I figured it was time. I'm coming up on thirty, and I truly want a family. But I've been having trouble getting pregnant. The longer it takes, the more I know this is what I want. I'm not sure Dylan feels the same way."

"Can't blame him," Maud said with a grin. "Most studs don't seem to care if they ever see the foals."

"He's not a horse. Or a prize bull."

"Of course not, kiddo. You're primates." Maude hugged her again. "If you're looking for a really good paternal role model, you might be better off emperor penguins."

"Penguins?"

"The baby's daddy hatches the egg."

Nicole couldn't help smiling back at her friend. "That's not a bad idea. Dylan really looks great in a tux."

"On a more serious note," Maud said, "you might consider talking to Sarah about your marriage."

"Why? Our relationship doesn't have anything to do with the kidnapping." Nicole frowned.

"But your marriage affects almost everything in your life. Right?"

"I've already tried to get Dylan to come with me to

a counselor." That was an epic argument. "He didn't like the idea."

"Try again." Maud gathered her close for another hug.

Was that really the best thing? Nicole wished she knew exactly what to do. Nothing seemed certain.

WHEN IT CAME to running the ranch, Dylan hated to be second-guessed. But he was more than happy to let Carolyn give the orders when it came to Christmas decorations.

She had assigned him the job of stringing popcorn and cranberries in a long garland to be draped on the tree. He sat on a sofa in the living room with bowls of fluffy white popcorn and berries on the coffee table in front of him. Though he didn't much like working with a needle and thread, he preferred the sidelines to Burke's job of hanging the lights on the tree under Carolyn's direct supervision. The big, tall FBI agent had silenced Dylan's sister more than once by scooping her off the floor and carrying her several feet away from the tree. He didn't seem to mind that she kept bouncing right back.

Jesse Longbridge had arrived with their neighbor, Fiona Grant, and her five-year-old daughter, Abby. Fiona was a potter, and she'd brought a boxful of hand-made ceramic elves, glazed in red and green.

In the past few days, Fiona and Jesse had clearly become a couple. Constantly touching, they couldn't take their eyes off each other.

Dylan remembered how it had been when he and Nicole had first fallen in love. A golden glow had surrounded them. Her laughter was music. Her touch was magic. When she'd looked at him with love shining from her blue eyes, she'd been the most beautiful woman in the world.

She still was. In his eyes, she was near perfect. Strong and healthy, she could ride for hours. During calving season, she worked harder than any man. But there was something ethereal about her, like an angel. She looked as delicate as a snowflake with her pale blond hair and her translucent skin. He didn't tell her that often enough.

Jesse crossed the room with a mug of coffee in his hand and took a seat on the chair beside the sofa. "I guess Christmas is a big deal around here. You've got more decorations than a shopping mall."

"It's Nicole's favorite season."

"How's she doing?"

"She seems okay." Dylan shrugged. "We'd all feel a lot better if Nate Miller was locked up behind bars."

Jesse sipped his coffee and licked his lips. "I only talked to Nate once. It was before we considered him to be a suspect, but I should have known he was up to something. The man's crazy. He blames your dad for his own father's death."

"He might have a point," Dylan said as he stabbed another cranberry with the needle.

"How so?"

"My dad offered old man Miller the chance to join us when we changed to organic ranching. When he refused, the Circle M started going downhill. Nobody wanted to buy what they were selling. Their herd got smaller and even less profitable. Ultimately, they lost everything. I can see how Nate would blame my dad for breaking his father's heart."

"A rational explanation," Jesse said. "Nate isn't that logical. He claims that Sterling actually killed his father."

Dylan hadn't heard this story before. "Old man Miller died of a heart attack."

"Nate told me that he heard your dad's voice from outside right before his father keeled over in one of the cattle pens and got trampled. In his version of the story, Sterling could have saved him if he'd called the ambulance."

"Crazy," Dylan muttered.

"But Nate believes it. In his twisted mind, he blames the Carlisles for the death of his father and for nearly losing his ranch, which is why he thinks his wife left him. And why he can't spend time with his kid."

"Everything bad that ever happened to him."

"That's the size of it," Jesse said. "He really hates you, Dylan. He's not going to stop coming after you."

"Well, Jesse, I guess we're going to need Longbridge Security until Nate gets arrested."

"I'm happy to stay in the area." He grinned as he looked toward Fiona and her daughter. "But I don't think bodyguards are going to solve your problem. In my professional opinion, you and Nicole and Carolyn should go somewhere else. Somewhere that Nate can't find you."

Jesse was the second person today to advise him to get out of town. This morning, the sheriff had said the only way he'd avoid the media was to leave. "I can't just take off. This ranch doesn't run itself. With Lucas dead, I don't even have a foreman."

Dylan sure as hell didn't like the idea of turning tail and running, being driven off his property by a polecat like Nate. Dammit, this was his home.

Glancing toward the hallway, he spotted Nicole walking beside Doc Maud. From across the room, he recognized the signs of tension in the way she held her shoulders. Her eyes seemed puffy. Had she been crying?

He hoped the doctor hadn't given her bad news. Even more, he hoped that Nicole wouldn't be ticked off because he'd gone behind her back to arrange for a check-up. She seemed to be avoiding him as she greeted their other guests, paying special attention to little Abby. The five-year-old's curly blond hair made her look more like Nicole than her own mother.

Dylan turned to Jesse. "You and Fiona?"

"She's a special lady." Jesse's grin spread wider. "I'm thinking of taking a leave of absence from the security guard business and staying with her for a while."

"Can you take time off? I thought you were the boss."

"I'm the founder of Longbridge Security, but my sister in Denver really runs things. She'll manage."

"We've got more in common than I thought," Dylan said. "We've both got take-charge sisters involved in our business."

"A blessing and a curse." Jesse raised his mug toward Carolyn who was fussing with the lights on the tree. "I wish Burke the best of luck."

"He's in for a wild ride," Dylan agreed.

On the far side of the living room, Nicole escorted Dylan's mother to the spinet against the wall that held framed photographs of generations of Carlisles, dating back to the early 1900s. Andrea was the only one in the family who played the piano, but Dylan still kept it well-maintained and tuned.

Nicole turned off the CD as Andrea began to play "Jingle Bells." It didn't take long for people to gather around the piano and start singing carols.

Jesse stood. "Think about what I said. It might be good for you and Nicole to get away from the ranch."

Dylan nodded. If the only way to keep Nicole safe was to run, he didn't have a choice.

## Chapter Ten

Before she'd been kidnapped, Nicole hadn't considered brushing her teeth to be a luxury. Going without a toothbrush for a week changed her mind. She brushed and rinsed and brushed again. The inside of her mouth tasted clean. Minty. Wonderful.

She bared her teeth and stared at her reflection in the bathroom mirror. Her face looked tired, pale and a bit feral, like a rabid squirrel. *Am I getting better?* Today should have been a time of good cheer, filled with friends, family and Christmas spirit. She'd made an effort to join the party. Singing carols. Drinking spiced cider. Lighting Christmas candles. Everyone had complimented her on her quick recovery from a terrible situation. They'd told her she looked good. They were happy for her.

But her fixed smile masked an underlying fear. Her laughter stifled an urge to scream.

On the counter beside the sink was the cell phone Dylan had given her. He'd thoughtfully programmed her most frequently called phone numbers with his cell listed as number one.

It was after nine o'clock. She still hadn't called Nate.

His whispered threats repeated endlessly in her mind. If she didn't do as he said, someone would suffer. She should return his call. *But, damn. I don't want to.* She rationalized that Nate wasn't all-powerful. Their ranch house was well-guarded. He couldn't get to her or her family. But she was still afraid.

Taking the cell phone with her, she opened the bathroom door. She should have been ready for sleep. Most ranchers were early to bed and early to rise. But she'd always been a bit of a night owl. As was her husband.

When they were first married, these hours between nine and midnight had been their special time. And it wasn't always about sex…frequently, but not always. With everyone else asleep, they'd sneak downstairs for a snack. Or go to his office, snuggle on the sofa and watch a favorite old movie on TV. She treasured those memories of intimacy. Lately, Dylan had been working so hard that he was sound asleep by nine.

Not tonight. He stood beside the bedroom window. His shoulders slouched a bit. His thumb hooked in the pocket of his jeans. Though she was wearing flannel pajamas, Dylan hadn't changed from his day clothes. They hadn't discussed tonight's sleeping arrangements.

"Is it snowing again?" she asked.

"There's a couple of lazy flakes drifting down. More in the forecast for tomorrow."

"Good," she said. "We'll have a white Christmas."

When she joined him at the window, he pulled her close against him and said, "Jesse told me that we're never supposed to stand directly in front of a window with the light shining behind us. We'd be easy targets for a sniper."

Her fingers tightened on the cell phone. Was Nate out

there? Was he watching? She tried to ease her tension with a laugh. "It'd take some fancy shooting to make that shot."

"It's better not to take chances." His low baritone rumbled as if he was speaking from deep inside himself. "I didn't leave the house all day. I can't remember ever doing that before, except for when I'm sick in bed."

She peeked around the edge of the window to gaze at the snow-covered rocks and hills in the wide mountain valley that spread toward Riverton and Delta. Lights twinkled from houses far away.

"One good thing," she said as she looked down at the gate in front of their property, "the television news truck is gone."

"I hate to say it, but they'll be back tomorrow. Carolyn says they aren't going to leave until you give an interview."

She shuddered. "No way."

His other arm encircled her, and her shoulder adjusted to fit neatly against his chest. His bodily warmth soothed and comforted her. "There are going to be stories," he said, "whether you talk to the reporters or not."

She tilted her chin to look up at him. "I can't talk about it. Not to strangers. There are things I don't even want to tell you."

"Like what?" His voice took on a sharp edge. The sinewy muscles in his arms flexed and tensed. "You can tell me anything, darlin'."

*Hadn't she just said that she preferred not to?* "It's nothing."

"He didn't touch you, did he?"

"Of course he did," she said impatiently. "He dragged me from here to there, threw me in the trunk of a car. Of course, there was physical contact."

"You know what I mean. Was there anything sexual?"

She was sure that, in her husband's mind, rape was the worst thing that could happen. Maybe it was. She couldn't say because that hadn't been her experience. "There was nothing like that. He didn't want anything to do with me."

His sigh of relief blew through her hair.

She shouldn't have been irritated. But it seemed as though he was suggesting that if she hadn't been raped, her captivity wasn't really all that terrible. *Why should you be so upset? You weren't molested, after all.* She wriggled free and moved away from him. "You don't get it."

"Darlin', I'm trying to understand."

"Forget it."

She turned away from him, walked the few paces to the bed and placed the cell phone on the bedside table. How could she explain what it was like to pee in a jar, to be chained like a dog, to pray for mercy that never came? Nate had broken her down. Waiting for him, hour after hour, she actually looked forward to his appearances. She craved the meager food and water he brought for her.

For a while, she'd wished for death. It would have been better to die with honor than live without self-respect. But she wanted to survive.

"We'll talk about something else," Dylan said.

He was smart enough not to approach her. If he tried to cuddle her and tell her that everything was all right, she might snap.

"The doctor," he said. "What did the doctor say when she examined you?"

"My injuries are superficial. No problem." She turned and faced him. "The way you used Maud was really devious. You knew I wouldn't refuse to see the doc if Maud was involved."

"Did she give you any medication?"

"I'm not putting any drugs into my system. Not while I'm trying to get pregnant."

"I understand."

*Did he?* She couldn't read his expression. Whenever they talked about having a baby, he seemed guarded—almost as if her big, strong husband was scared.

"The doctor's name is Sarah." Nicole watched for his reaction as she said, "She's a psychiatrist."

His eyebrows shot up. His mouth gaped like a bass, then popped shut. It was safe to assume that he was surprised by this bit of information. Stunned, even. "What the hell was Maud thinking? You need a real doctor."

"Sarah has medical training. Her examination was thorough, and she took some blood samples. Mostly, we talked."

Dylan paced at the far end of the room. Obviously, he hadn't expected a shrink. When he cleared his throat, it sounded like the growl of a grizzly. "Great, just great. If she can help, I'm all for it."

"That's a change of attitude. As I recall, you were opposed to marriage counseling."

"Twice a week, driving all the way to Delta. I don't have time."

They'd had this argument before—a familiar tune played in a discordant key. "You wouldn't even try."

"All we'd do with a counselor is talk, and we can do that right here. Right now. Look at the two of us. You see? We're talking."

She sank onto the bed. "And this is such a magical conversation."

There was a knock on the door, and Carolyn called out, "Are you awake?"

Simultaneously, Dylan and Nicole said, "Come in."

Dylan's sister swept into the room, wearing her bathrobe and a nightshirt that looked suspiciously like the top of a pair of men's extra-extra-large pajamas. "The sheriff called. He tried to reach you first, Dylan, but your phone's turned off. So is mine. But Burke always keeps the line of communication open, and—"

"Carolyn," Dylan interrupted, "why did he call?"

"Before I say anything else, I don't want you to panic. Neither of you."

A knot tightened in the center of Nicole's chest. Something terrible had happened. She looked toward the cell phone resting on her bedside table. "What is it, Carolyn?"

"There was a break-in at Maud's veterinary clinic. Windows were broken. Computers were smashed. The file cabinets were trashed."

"The animals?" Nicole leapt to her feet. "Are the animals all right?"

"Yes," Carolyn said. "A couple of the dogs wouldn't stop howling. That's why the sheriff's office was called."

"I don't understand," Nicole said. "Maud has an alarm system. She's been vandalized before by people trying to break into her drug cabinet."

"The alarm was disabled," Carolyn said. "The sheriff said it was a neat bit of electrical work."

*The sort of work a handyman could do. A handyman like Nate Miller.* Nicole saw Carolyn fidget. There was something else that she wasn't saying. "What is it?"

"There was a spray-painted message on the wall. It said, 'I won't stop.' The signature was an *M* in a circle."

Circle M. Nate told her that if she didn't do as he ordered, he'd go after the people she loved. Now he'd made good on that threat. The vandalism at Maud's clinic was her fault. All her fault.

Though her heart beat faster than a hummingbird's wings, she kept her exterior calm as she picked up her cell phone. "I need to call Maud and see if there's anything I can do."

As soon as Dylan left the bedroom, Nicole knew what she must do. All day long she'd avoided making the call to Nate. She'd been pretending, hoping, wishing with all her heart that his threats would somehow go away.

She'd been wrong.

And Maud had paid the price.

Dylan had freed her from the chains Nate had used to keep her captive, but terror was an even stronger cage.

She sat in the middle of the bed, assailed by flashbacks of screaming until her throat was raw, struggling against the handcuffs, fighting her hunger and her thirst. Her fading bruises throbbed with renewed pain. The gummy taste of duct tape coated her mouth.

She'd feared for her own survival. But even more important was the safety of the people she loved. When she'd had her meeting with Dylan, she would have chosen death rather than deny her love for him. But he had been in danger, too. If she hadn't followed the script, Dylan would have been killed.

She had to protect him. And Maud. And everyone else she cared about. *But do I have to do it alone?*

Not telling Dylan about the contact from Nate was like lying to him, and she hated the way it felt. Nate had driven a wedge between them.

Determined to put an end to this sick connection, she called the number Nate had given her. The phone range six times before he picked up.

"You're late," he whispered.

"You shouldn't have gone after Maud."

"Got your attention, didn't I?"

*Bastard!* "If you hurt anyone else, I won't cooperate."

"Don't try to bargain, Nicole. I'm in charge, and you'll do what I tell you to do."

She had no leverage. Her resistance felt weak. "Why should I? How do I know you won't come after Dylan?"

"You don't," he said. "But if you don't follow my orders, I promise that you won't like the results. The next time I won't be satisfied with destroying property. I will take lives. Your friends, your family, all your pretty little horses. Do you believe me?"

"Yes." All her fear came rushing back. She gained nothing by fighting. He was capable of terrible violence.

"Tell no one that you're in contact with me."

She had no choice. She had to lie. A helpless sob crawled up her throat. *Dylan, I'm sorry.*

"Nicole, did you hear me?"

"Tell me what I have to do."

DYLAN LEFT Nicole alone in the bedroom to make her phone call and went downstairs to the kitchen. Though he felt bad about Maud's clinic, Carolyn's interruption had come at the right time. He didn't want to get rolling with a bunch of tired old arguments.

Trips into Delta twice a week to see a counselor? It didn't fit his schedule. And he didn't need an outside person telling him how to run his life.

He moved quietly through the house, not needing to turn on any of the lights. This had been his home since he was born. Except for college in Fort Collins, he'd never lived anywhere else. Just like his dad.

Sure, there were similarities between him and his old man, and it wasn't all bad. They were both ranchers, good providers, conscious of the environment. And they both had trouble in their marriage.

Dylan had learned a lesson by watching his father. Sterling had never found another woman he loved as much as Andrea. He'd gone through life alone. *I won't make the same mistake.* If Nicole needed for him to see a shrink, he'd do it. By God, he'd do any damn thing to save his marriage.

In the kitchen, he took a half gallon of milk from the fridge and poured himself a glass. A shot of whiskey might go down well, but he wanted to stay alert in case Nicole had another rough night.

Through the kitchen window, he saw hillsides covered with pristine white snow. The smells of pine boughs and gingerbread lingered from the afternoon.

From the front room, he heard the spinet. Not a Christmas song, but a sonata. The music took him back in time to when he was a little boy, sitting beside his mom on the piano bench, listening as her long fingers stroked the keys.

Quietly, he went through the dining room. In the living room, the lights flickered on the Christmas tree. Andrea sat with her back to him, making music.

He'd never forgiven her for leaving him and Carolyn, for choosing to follow her own dreams. But he'd never stopped loving his mother. He came up behind her. "Don't stop playing."

"Do you remember?" she asked.

He hesitated for a long moment. "I remember, Mom."

He hadn't called her Mom in a hell of a long time. But it felt right. Standing behind her, he listened and thought of how much he'd missed by being too stubborn to return her gestures when she reached out to him.

"You've never asked me for advice," she said, continuing to play. "But I have something to say."

"I'm ready to hear it."

"You and Nicole are soul mates. You're meant to be together. But she's been badly hurt. You're going to have to fight to win her back."

"Fight?" If it meant saving his marriage, he was ready to kick ass. Preferably, Nate Miller's ass. But he was pretty sure that wasn't what Andrea meant. "How am I supposed to do that?"

"You need to court her. The roses were a good start, but you need to do more." Her fingers darted across the keys, unleashing a cascade of notes. "My advice is to take her away from the ranch. Go somewhere special. Just the two of you. Spend some time together without interruptions, and use that time to show her how much you care."

She was the third person to advise him to get out of town, but he liked her reasoning more than the sheriff's or Jesse's. Taking Nicole somewhere special for a second honeymoon sounded a lot better than running from Nate Miller or hiding from the media.

He reached down and rested his hand on Andrea's shoulder. "Thanks."

She stopped playing and looked up at him. In the reflected light from the Christmas tree, her eyes were bright. "I love you, son."

He leaned down and kissed her cheek. "Love you, Mom."

## Chapter Eleven

The next morning Dylan was up early again, taking care of business, pacing back and forth from his office to the kitchen. He'd spent much of last night watching his wife sleep restlessly—not touching her, except to rearrange the comforter and soothe away the nightmares. He wanted more. A lot more. His desire for her had built to an almost painful level. If this went on much longer, he'd be driven into a drooling, primitive state of pure lust. *Dylan the Caveman.* He'd club his woman over the head, drag her off and make sweet love.

When he heard Nicole come down the stairs, he grabbed two mugs of coffee and whisked her into his office, where he closed the door. He wasted no time with explanations.

"We need to leave the ranch."

Coolly, she raised her coffee mug to her lips and gazed at him over the brim. "Did I miss something? Is the building on fire?"

"The sheriff says we won't to be able to avoid the press if we stay here. Jesse says we aren't safe." He shuffled his feet, reluctant to confess the most important part of his plan: to woo her. "Also, we need some alone time.

You and me. Without distractions. Kind of like a second honeymoon."

For their first honeymoon they'd gone to Hawaii for a week. The lush green islands had enchanted him. He'd never forget the sight of his beautiful wife wading through the surf with rivulets of water streaming from her body.

Thoughtfully she sipped her coffee. "Have you heard anything more from Maud?"

"I talked to her this morning. She's fine. Her insurance will cover the vandalism."

"That's what she said last night." Avoiding his gaze, she crossed the office to the window and looked out. "Any word from the sheriff?"

"He's certain that Nate was responsible for the break-in at Maud's clinic. His fingerprints were all over."

"As if the Circle M painted on the wall wasn't proof enough?"

"Sheriff Trainer will stop by today and give us an update." Placing his mug on the desk, he came up behind her. Lightly, he touched her arm. "Come away with me, darlin'."

"Did you have a location in mind for this second honeymoon?"

"Actually, I do. It's a historical place."

"Europe?" She spun around to face him. "I've always wanted to go to Paris and see the Eiffel Tower. I could finish up my Christmas shopping there."

"Ooh-la-la," he said.

As quickly as her enthusiasm appeared, it faded into a frown. "But Paris is too far away. I'd rather be home for Christmas."

"Not Europe," he said. "For this vacation, you need to pack your bathing suit."

"Like Hawaii." Her blue eyes turned dreamy. "Our first honeymoon was amazing."

They'd made love in the morning, the night and all the hours in between. He remembered how the tropical breezes caressed his senses. Every sky held a rainbow. With a tinge of regret, he said, "Not a tropical island."

"Baja. The Sea of Cortez," she guessed. "We could swim with the dolphins. But the best time to go there is February or March when the whales are migrating. The photos show them swimming right up to the edge of the boats. You can reach out and—"

He held up a hand to stop her before she went too far down this path. "Not Baja. Not an island. I want to stay close to home in case there's trouble and we need to get back."

"I thought the whole idea was to run away to a place where no one could find us."

His whole idea was to seduce her, to remind her of their love—the passion they shared. "No one will find us."

"Where?"

"Glenwood," he said. "The hot springs at Glenwood."

Cynically she arched an eyebrow. "That's your idea of a second honeymoon? Glenwood Springs is less than a hundred miles from here."

He'd been thinking of her bruises when the idea of the medicinal hot springs occurred to him. Soaking in a steamy bath would be good for her. "You've said before that you wanted to go there."

"True, but you jacked my expectations way high." She shrugged and went around the desk toward the door. "It's a nice idea, Dylan."

*Nice?* That wasn't the response he was looking for. He'd hoped for wild excitement, hoped that she'd leap into his arms and kiss him for being so thoughtful. "Paris isn't out of the question."

"I don't mean to be so difficult." A deep sadness tainted her smile. "All I really want is to spend Christmas here at the ranch with you."

He followed as she sauntered from the office and went to the living room where she stood in front of the Christmas tree. Reaching up, she touched a teardrop-shaped ornament that was handpainted with a picture of a cowgirl on a horse. She'd told him the story of how her mother had given her that battered ornament when she was a little girl.

With a sigh, she looked toward another ornament. Her slender hand cupped the shiny globe hanging at eye-level. "This is the first ornament you gave me."

He'd chosen it with care. A dramatic tracery of black ran through blended colors—gold, red and magenta. It reminded him of a western sunset. "My horizon."

On the lower branches of the tree was the ornament he'd given her last year—a shiny Santa that he'd grabbed as an afterthought on a shopping trip to Grand Junction. The design meant nothing special.

"Even if I agree to leave," she said, "how would we get away from the ranch unnoticed? That stupid press truck is parked at the front gate."

He'd given their escape route some thought, had even consulted with his sister and Burke. "You're right. We can't just hop in the truck and drive off without being followed."

"Then what do you suggest?"

The decorated boughs of the Christmas tree sparkled behind her. The lights and tinsel highlighted the gleam of her blond hair. This incredible, beautiful woman was his wife. And he wanted her. He'd do just about anything to get her alone.

"Chopper," he said.

"Fly to Glenwood on a helicopter?"

"Not directly. We'd fly from one airfield to another until we reach the Eagle County Airport near Vail. From there, we pick up a rental car, reserved under an alias."

"An alias?"

"Well, we can't use our own name. The media would find us for sure. Then we drive to Glenwood Springs, where our hotel room is being held under the alias."

"This is beginning to sound like high espionage."

"Burke helped me with the details." Having an FBI agent in the family was proving useful. "Nobody will know who we are. Especially since we'll be wearing disguises."

"Come again?"

In his opinion, this was the best part. "There's always a chance that we'll run into somebody we know. And Burke said that reporters might talk to hotel clerks and show them a photograph. So we need to be disguised."

"How?"

"You could be a redhead. With lots of makeup and cleavage."

"You want me to dress up like a bimbo?"

"Because that's the very opposite of who you really are," he said quickly. "I figure you could play the part of my sexpot mistress. And I'd be a hotshot business-man. Maybe an attorney. I could wear a fake mustache and a silk necktie."

"Oh, yeah. That'll work."

His fantasy about their disguises went far beyond putting on costumes. "Maybe we should practice."

"I can tell that you've put a lot of thought into this," she said. "Clearly, you shouldn't be left alone in the morning—you seem to come up with all kinds of schemes."

If he'd been getting a decent night's sleep in his wife's arms, he wouldn't have all this excess energy. "We need to leave the ranch until this is over."

"I'm sorry, but no. We'll stay here and ride it out."

She turned on her heel and marched into the kitchen.

NICOLE CLENCHED her jaw to keep from crying. Walking away from Dylan was hard, really hard. Her feet dragged across the floor as if she were fighting a powerful magnet that pulled her back toward his arms.

His crazy, intricate scheme for a getaway touched her heart. For months, she'd felt as though he barely noticed her existence. And now, when he'd gone to extreme lengths and arranged *everything* with her in mind, she had to reject him.

Nate gave her no other choice. He'd given her a simple assignment for today. If she failed to do his bidding, others would suffer. She wondered how he'd know when she carried out the task. *Is he watching the ranch house right now?* Last night, while she lay in bed pretending to sleep, she considered telling Dylan about her phone call to Nate. They could set a trap for him.

But if she was wrong… If they failed to catch him, there would be hell to pay. She didn't dare take the risk.

In the kitchen, she put on a perfunctory smile for Polly. Unaware of what she was saying, Nicole nodded and chatted while Polly put together a breakfast of sausage and eggs wrapped in a tortilla.

It looked good. Nicole leaned against the counter

and took a bite. *Yum.* Civilized people sat at the table and used silverware, but Nicole was just too hungry.

"Snow's already given up," Polly said. "I guess those forecasters were wrong."

"Guess so," Nicole said.

The plump, energetic woman bustled around the large kitchen. Her every move was precise—as choreographed as a ballet. "I think I'll be making some chili for lunch."

Before Nicole could finish the last bite of her breakfast burrito, her stomach roiled. "Excuse me, Polly."

"What's the matter, hon? You look sick."

"I'll be back later. To help." She dashed into the small downstairs bathroom. Bracing her arms on the counter beside the sink, she fought the urge to vomit. A sickening fever surged through her, and she broke into a clammy sweat. Though she was certain that her reaction was psychological, she kind of hoped it was a virus. Collapsing into bed with the flu seemed way more acceptable than admitting that she was too scared to eat or sleep or make love to her husband.

Dammit. She had to figure out how to follow Nate's orders without getting caught. He'd told her to go to the stable that had been burned down. At the northeast corner she'd find a leather pouch. She was supposed to keep it with her at all times.

The task would have been simple if she hadn't been surrounded by ranch hands and bodyguards. And Dylan. He'd never let her stroll out of the ranch house alone. She'd have to come up with an excuse; she'd have to lie to him.

Her stomach heaved, she vomited into the toilet bowl. She felt like hell. It wouldn't be malingering if she claimed to be sick and unable to leave her bed. Would Nate believe that excuse?

She slipped out of the bathroom and scurried up the stairs to the sanctuary of her bedroom. After a few minutes' rest, nervous energy compelled her to rise from the bed. She paced. *Tell Dylan about the contact from Nate.* They could use Burke's and Jesse's expertise to figure out a plan. Nate wasn't a genius. He couldn't outsmart them all.

But he was good at plotting and hiding. And he was driven by an all-consuming need for revenge.

She grabbed one of the energy bars in her room and nibbled at it while she stood at the window. A fluffy blanket of snow covered the landscape. Only a couple of inches. The sun was out today. Most of the snow would be melted by nightfall.

When she finished off the energy bar, she checked in with her stomach. Though tense, she didn't feel like throwing up. Was she sick? Or was she crazy? As Sarah had easily diagnosed, Nicole had been traumatized. After what she'd been through, there had to be an emotional reaction.

From downstairs, she heard people moving around in the house. It was after ten o'clock; the day's activities were under way. On a normal day, she would have been busy with the daily chores she loved— feeding the livestock, mucking out the horse barn, monitoring the herd. For the past several months, she'd been participating in a study sponsored by the veterinary college in Grand Junction that required her to draw blood from the cattle. Which reminded her that she ought to call Sarah and ask for preliminary results on her own blood tests.

But when she picked up the cell phone, she was reminded of Nate. She stared at the innocent rectangle of plastic and circuits and wires. It was more than a phone. This was a link to him. Another chain. *What the hell could she do to stop him?*

He had trapped her here. The walls seemed to close around her more tightly than those of the dark closet where she'd been held prisoner. She wanted to run. To get away from here. *Wasn't that exactly what Dylan had suggested?* Taking off with him and going to Glenwood sounded like the answer to her prayers.

There was a tap on the door, and she closed her eyes, pretending to sleep so she wouldn't have to face another person or come up with another lie. The door opened. Through slitted eyelids, she saw Carolyn step inside, give her a look and leave.

After a few minutes, she tiptoed to the window, trying to determine the best route to leave the house and go to the burned stable. Two ranch hands were posted at the front gate, and she knew there were another two on the porch—too many people who would ask questions or insist on accompanying her.

She spotted the sheriff's SUV parked near the front. Carolyn must have come to the door to tell her that the sheriff was here, which meant that she and Burke *and* Dylan would be busy hearing Sheriff Trainer's report. They'd all be locked up together in Dylan's office.

This was her chance to slip outside.

She threw on a heavy sweater from her closet. If she put on more obvious outdoor clothing, somebody would stop her from leaving the house. They had their orders.

And she had hers.

She crept down the stairs and dodged through the house, ducking around corners to avoid being seen. *This was crazy!* But it was more insane to disobey Nate. No telling who he'd attack next.

Closing the back door behind her, she slipped outside. The cool, fresh air washed over her, arousing her senses. The glitter of sunlight on snow dazzled her. For a moment, she forgot her mission and reveled in the pure joy of being outside.

She needed this. Nicole had always been an outdoors person. She loved the whispering wind and the taste of moisture in the air. This was what she needed. This was her cure.

Just then, the young cowboy MacKenzie came around the corner of the house, and she darted toward the trunk of a cottonwood near the house. He didn't see her.

Down the sloping path, she ran. Her feet felt light. Not even breathing hard, she circled the bunkhouse and leaned against the wall on the side away from the house. From this vantage point, she could see the stable that had burned. One of the older buildings on the property, it wasn't a great loss in terms of the structure itself. But the fire had destroyed a lot of equipment and tack— saddles, bridles and halters.

The charred remains of the stable walls contrasted with the pure-white snow. She stared at the corner Nate had designated. What had he hidden there? A map? A key? A gun? If it was something lethal, like a bomb, there was no way she'd put others in danger.

When had he taken the risk of coming so close to the house? Yesterday when everyone was inside, talking and laughing and decorating the Christmas tree? His approach must have been at least a day ago—long enough for the wind to erase his footprints in the snow.

She hurried down the hill. The exhilaration of physical movement mingled with her fear—a giddy combination. The inside of her head was spinning. Which corner had he told her? Northwest or northeast?

Her gaze lit on a dark leather pouch, half buried in snow. As she picked it up, she scanned the surrounding forest. Was Nate nearby, watching them from a snipers perch? Had she been lured into a trap?

## Chapter Twelve

Dylan strode the last few paces toward his wife. What the hell was she thinking? Leaving the house to go out onto the porch would have been dangerous enough. But here? Standing in the snow with nothing to protect her, she was easy prey. He looked toward the trees, half expecting to see the gleam of sunlight on gunmetal.

His hand slapped his hip, reaching for a holster that wasn't there. The whole time she'd been missing, he'd been armed. But not today. Not when he might really need his weapon.

As he approached, she sank to her knees, breathing hard. Though she waved him off, it seemed like a struggle for her to stagger to her feet. She faced him. "I'm sorry, Dylan."

"Did you forget what happened the last time you went running off by yourself?"

"Of course not." Her voice was firm, but she wavered on her feet. "How did you find me?"

He pointed to the snow behind him. "You left a trail a blind man could follow."

"So I did. I guess…" Her voice trailed off. Her knees sagged.

He stepped forward and caught her before she fainted onto the charred earth beside the burned stable. Her weakness might be a blessing in disguise. He wouldn't have to waste time arguing with her about why they needed to get back to the house.

From a distance, he heard the lowing of cattle. Overhead, a hawk circled and screeched. *Was there a movement in the forest?*

If Dylan had been alone, he'd have welcomed the opportunity for a showdown with Nate. But Nicole was with him.

With adrenaline charging through his veins, he easily found the strength to carry her up the slope. It was vital to find shelter, to get her inside where she'd be out of harm's way. As he made tracks across the snow-covered field, the back of his neck prickled. At any moment, a gunshot could ring out. They'd both be dead, and Nate would have his revenge.

Near the bunkhouse, she fidgeted in his arms. Her eyelids were open. "You can put me down."

"Planning to run off again?"

"Please, Dylan." Her tone gave him pause; she almost seemed to be begging him. "Haven't I been embarrassed enough? I don't want to be carried into the house like a child."

Protected by the eaves of the bunkhouse, he lowered her legs to the ground. His arm still supported most of her weight as he looked down into her blue eyes, checking for signs of further weakness. "Are you all right?"

"I'm not going to collapse again."

"Dammit, Nicole. You scared the crap out of me."

When he'd realized that she wasn't in the house, he'd

panicked. Losing her again would drive him straight over the edge.

"I didn't mean to worry you," she said. "I just wanted to catch a breath of fresh air."

"Nate could be anywhere," he warned. "We can't take chances."

She nodded. "I understand."

*Did she? Did she, really?* Her glib, easy response fueled his anger. Clearly, she didn't understand a damned thing. She didn't know what was best for her, best for them.

He had to take charge. Whether or not she liked it.

"We're going to Glenwood," he said. "We can't stay here, being held prisoner in our own house. Don't even think about arguing."

Her lips pinched together. "Is that an order?"

"Damn right."

He hustled her back toward the house. Earlier, when he'd found her missing, he hadn't raised an alarm. His brain had been too full of disaster scenarios to make any kind of sensible plan. He'd acted on instinct to find her.

When they got inside, Carolyn glared at him. "Where were you?"

"I need for you to make those arrangements," he said. "The ones we talked about earlier."

"The chopper?"

Dylan nodded. "That's right. The sooner we can get started, the better."

"Done," she said.

He marched Nicole up the staircase to their bedroom and closed the door. "Get packed."

"Is there any room for compromise?"

He knew what that meant. During the years of their

marriage, they'd developed a system of decision-making. Some situations were obvious, based on their personal likes and dislikes. She never expected him to sit through chick flicks with her. And he'd resigned himself to the fact that she wouldn't accompany him on hunting trips. As a veterinarian, she'd probably try to revive any animal—even a coyote—that he shot.

For more complicated matters, they each made a list of pluses and minuses. When they compared notes, the final decision was usually obvious.

"We aren't making a list, Nicole. Not this time."

"I fainted," she pointed out. "If I'm really sick, I don't want to leave home."

"If you're ill, we'll take you to a hospital in Denver for treatment. With Longbridge Security guards posted outside your room."

A frown creased her forehead. He could tell that she was irritated by not having her opinion considered, but that was too damned bad. He wasn't taking any more chances.

She crossed the room to the dresser, where he'd left a cardboard box. "What's this?"

"Lucas Mann," he said. "Those are his ashes."

He'd intended to be gentle when he gave her the remains. He knew that she cared about the old foreman, maybe even looked upon him as a father figure. Good fathers seemed to be in short supply around here.

Her fingers trailed across the cardboard surface. "Did the sheriff bring this?"

"Yes," he said tersely.

"I miss Lucas."

The sentimental note in her voice irked him. "We'll deal with the remains later."

She turned toward him. Her eyes were moist. He couldn't take much more of her moodiness. What the hell was wrong with her?

"Get packed, Nicole."

He turned on his heel and left the room before he exploded and said something he would surely regret.

THE SLAM of their bedroom door punctuated her husband's anger. Nicole couldn't blame him. She'd crept out of the house and broken the rules put in place by people who wanted only to keep her safe.

It was small comfort that she'd successfully completed her objective before she keeled over. She took the leather pouch from the pocket of her sweater. Not wanting to be caught with whatever Nate had left for her, she went into the bathroom and locked the door. Hiding again.

Everything she did, every move she made seemed to be a fresh betrayal of Dylan. She couldn't continue to act this way. Every deception felt like a dark seed that took root in her soul and grew, sprouting vines that would strangle and destroy her marriage. Sooner or later, she had to tell him the whole truth.

There were practical reasons for coming clean. Because she'd been following Nate's instructions, Dylan had been in danger. If Nate had been lurking in the forest, he could have opened fire.

*But how can I tell him?* If she revealed too much, Dylan might never look at her with love in his eyes. He'd only see a pathetic victim.

She loosened the strings on the pouch. Inside was a small rectangular device that would fit easily into a pocket. A GPS locator. Nate wanted to monitor her location. Once again, she was his captive.

GPS locators could be purchased from several locations, but they weren't cheap. Nate must have tapped into the money he'd taken from the ransom—Carlisle money that Lucas Mann had died trying to protect.

Using the cell phone, she called the number he'd given her. This time he answered quickly. "Yes, Nicole."

"I did as you told me."

"Turn it on," he whispered.

Her finger poised on the switch. There was absolutely no reason she had to play fair with Nate. She'd been lying to everybody else. It was Nate's turn.

She didn't want to talk to him anymore today. Or tomorrow. What she needed was an excuse. She activated the device. "Is it working?"

"Yes," he hissed. "Keep it on at all times. And keep it with you."

"I'll do as you say." Though she continued to play the role of the hapless captive, a plan formed in her mind. A way to outsmart him. "Not that I expect to be moving around too much."

"Why not?"

The mere fact that he'd asked a question gave her confidence. She exhaled a prolonged sigh. "You must have seen what happened when I went to the burned stable."

After a few seconds' hesitation, he said, "I see everything."

"Then you know that I collapsed. I had to be carried back to the house." She made her voice sound scratchy. "I'm terribly weak. I probably won't be leaving my bed."

"But I have another task."

"The doctor…" She breathed heavily into the cell phone. "The doctor gave me some medication. Can't move."

"Stop taking the sedatives."

For the first time, his voice rose above a creepy whisper. She could tell that he was agitated. His scheme didn't leave room for her to refuse him.

"Sleep." She groaned. "I must sleep."

"If you don't do as I say—"

"I'll try." Purposely, she dropped the cell phone on the carpet and fumbled while picking it up. "Can't move. Too weak. I have to hang up. I'll call you later."

With a small sense of triumph, she disconnected the call. If she was too ill to leave her bed, she couldn't possibly be expected to carry out his sick plans.

She took the GPS locator into her room and stashed it behind the bedside table. There it would stay. For once, she might have gotten the best of Nate Miller.

But there was still the problem of Dylan and his insistence on leaving the ranch. Taking off in a chopper was a dramatic exit. Even if Nate wasn't watching, word would get out.

She looked down at the cell phone in her hand. If she was going to use illness as an excuse, it might be a good idea to check in with Doctor Sarah. Maybe come up with a couple of fake symptoms to tell Nate about.

Sitting on the edge of her bed, she punched in the phone number for the clinic where Sarah worked and identified herself to the receptionist. She was put on hold. To tell the truth, the fainting worried Nicole. She had a strong constitution and wasn't prone to blackouts. It would be both horrible and ironic if her lie to Nate turned out to be the truth.

"This is Doctor Sarah Lowell."

"I'm glad I caught you," Nicole said. "I've been having a few problems. A few minutes ago, I fainted."

"How did you sleep last night?"

"Not well." She remembered waking up two or three times. And lying awake. Though she'd been in the bed for a full eight hours, she didn't feel well-rested. "Could I be suffering from exhaustion?"

"You're pretty good at self-diagnosis. When you fainted, were you doing something physical? Or stressful?"

*Walking across a field, expecting to be shot?* "You might say it was an intense situation."

"Are you still nauseous?"

"I vomited again this morning." Though she didn't really feel sick, there were enough symptoms to indicate something was wrong. Maybe she really did need a hospital. "I know it's early, but do you have the lab results from my blood work?"

"I have some preliminary results." Sarah paused. "Are you sitting down?"

Nervously, Nicole chewed on her lower lip. *Are you sitting down?* That was the line she used with pet owners before delivering bad news. "What is it, Sarah?"

"According to your blood work, you're pregnant."

Nicole gasped. Pregnant? That changed everything.

## Chapter Thirteen

Dylan had no idea why Nicole had gone from obstinate to cooperative in the blink of an eye. Instead of fighting him about the trip to Glenwood, she'd added her own spin to their getaway plan. They'd tell the reporters and everybody else who didn't know that Nicole was sick in bed—unable to leave the house, see anyone or give any sort of statement.

Carolyn didn't agree. Her irritation was obvious as she leaned against the closed door of their bedroom, watching while they packed. "That story doesn't make any sense."

"I like it," Nicole said as she held up a sleek blue bathing suit. "I wonder if this still fits. I've lost some weight."

"Buy a new one when you get there," Carolyn said.

"Telling people I'm sick solves all kinds of problems," Nicole said. "Nobody will be searching for us. Dylan and I won't have to be looking over our shoulders."

"It won't work," Carolyn grumbled.

Dylan knew his control-freak sister well enough to understand that her real problem was that she hadn't come up with the sick-in-bed scenario herself. "I suppose you have a better idea?"

"Do I have to do everything?" She threw her hands in the air. "I already arranged for the chopper to fly from one place to another. You've got your cover story and phony names."

"Burke took care of that part," Dylan said.

After a few phone calls and some fancy work on the computer, Special Agent Burke had set them up with fake identities and an equally fake credit card that operated like a real one—pulling money from the Carlisle accounts.

Dylan's alias was John Hellman, an elite Denver attorney. Nicole would be his mistress, Francis Montana.

"We're Frankie and Johnny," Nicole said with a grin. "I love Burke's sense of humor."

"Yeah, he's a hoot," Carolyn said. "I hope you know that I had to pull some strings to get you a very nice room."

"At the Lodge," he said. "Right?"

"Better," she said.

He never liked the way she bulldozed through with her decisions. "Better? How?"

"At the Lodge, you'd have to deal with a lot of people. Desk clerks, maids and other guests. I booked you into a very exclusive condo only a couple of blocks away from the Lodge."

"But I was looking forward to a midnight swim."

"No problem. Guests at the condo have twenty-four hour privileges at the pool."

Nicole shivered. "Swimming in the middle of the night? What's the big deal with this pool, anyway?"

"It's pretty damn spectacular. As big as two city blocks. Heated by hot-springs mineral water to a temperature of ninety-two degrees. And the soaking pool is ten degrees warmer."

"Like swimming in a bathtub," Nicole said.

"The biggest bathtub in the world."

"Yeah, yeah, yeah," Carolyn said. "Would you two please focus? Concentrate."

"On what?"

"Hold on." She pressed a hand to her forehead. "I'm getting a brainstorm."

Of course, she would. His big sister always had to run the show. Even when they were kids, she bossed him around—until he'd grown taller and stronger than she was. "Let's hear it."

"We can hide Nicole inside a big box or a trunk, and carry her out to the chopper."

He glanced toward his wife and saw a flash of panic cross her face. Part of the time she was held captive, she'd been locked in the trunk of a car. He didn't want to put her through that kind of experience again. "I don't like it."

"Why not?" she demanded.

"I just don't."

"Then you come up with something."

Both women stared at him. Carolyn scowled. Nicole had hope in her eyes; she believed in him. And he wouldn't disappoint her.

"More disguises," he said. "During the past week, we've had plenty of helicopters flying in and out of here. At one point, there were three FBI choppers, touching down and taking off. Plus dozens of agents coming and going. If Nicole and I both dress in black, we can say we're FBI agents returning to Denver."

"Works for me," Nicole said.

She gave him a glowing smile unlike anything he'd seen since her rescue. Radiant as a sunbeam. Full of life.

An hour later, when he climbed into the chopper beside her, she was still happy and excited. She motioned for Jesse to climb into the chopper with them.

"Nate is still out there, Jesse. You'll protect Fiona and her daughter, won't you?"

"With my life," he said. "Have a safe trip."

Moments later, the chopper lifted off. The eagle's-eye view of their ranch never failed to astound Dylan. Hundreds of snow-covered acres spread from pasture to forest to rocky crags. The chopper veered north, and he saw part of the herd—his herd, Carlisle Certified Organic Beef. Damn, they were pretty. The blocky shapes of heavy Black Angus cattle faded to dots as they swept through the clear skies of late afternoon.

Nicole sat close beside him on a bench seat. Though they were both wearing harness seat belts, she leaned so her body pressed against him as she looked down. She spoke loudly over the whir of the rotor, "I feel so free. This was a brilliant plan."

"I know."

He kissed her sweet, soft lips. The thrill reminded him of their first kiss so many years ago. Perfect happiness. This was the way his life was supposed to be.

They put on headsets to protect their ears from prolonged exposure to the noise of the chopper, and they had attached microphones so they could talk. But there wasn't much need for words. They rested in comfortable silence.

Nicole snuggled against him as they flew from one airfield to another. By the time they approached the twin peaks of Mount Sopris, sunset colored the skies. White snow carved with heavy purple shadows reached down toward the shimmering lights of mountain towns. The horizon surrounded them as they flew toward their destiny.

THE HELICOPTER set down at the Eagle County Airport near Vail. As Nicole disembarked, her hand rested protectively on her belly. A new life was growing inside her. A baby! They were going to have a baby. She wanted to wait until exactly the right moment to spring the joyful news. Her announcement would be a moment that she and Dylan would treasure for the rest of their lives.

To be sure, she didn't want to tell him while she had on her new disguise as Frankie Montana. She'd changed in the chopper. This outfit was a little bit country, and a whole lot trashy.

It had been hard to find anything suitable in her wardrobe. Her only low-cut top was a white leather vest that she usually wore over a T-shirt. No such modesty for Frankie! The vest buttoned just high enough to cover her bra, showing a hint of cleavage. Not that there was much to show. With pregnancy, her breasts would swell. She was pretty sure Dylan would enjoy that part of the process.

She still had on the slim black skirt she'd worn to look like an FBI agent, but had rolled the waist to make it a mini. Carolyn had suggested fishnet stockings and high heels, but the best Nicole could find in her closet was a pair of sheer black nylons and her dress-up cowboy boots in turquoise blue with white butterflies.

On top of it all, she wore a fringed leather jacket.

Before they entered the terminal, she spread her arms and twirled. "How do I look?"

"Like a cowgirl gone wild." He focused on her cleavage. "I wouldn't mind too much if you dressed like this all the time."

"Don't get your hopes up."

"I expected more makeup," he said. "Lots of stuff around your eyes."

"If I'd tried to put on lipstick in the chopper, I would have smeared it all over my face." The end result would have been more crazy than sexy. "It's not fair that you have to go to hardly any trouble at all. Just your black suit and a silk necktie."

"And these." He reached into his suit coat pocket and pulled out a pair of black-framed glasses he sometimes wore for reading. He perched them on his nose.

"Not much of a disguise," she said.

"Seems to work just fine for superheroes."

She reached up and took the glasses off. "Now, you're Dylan Carlisle, responsible rancher and cowboy." Then she put them back on. "Now, you're Johnny Hellman, sleazy attorney."

"Either way, I'm crazy about you."

He leaned down and kissed her again.

A pleasant ripple of excitement spilled through her. They had exchanged more gentle kisses and fond touches during their helicopter ride than they had in the months before she was kidnapped. Their regular lives had seemed too busy for holding hands or cuddling. Though their lovemaking had still been satisfying, it'd been different from when they first went to bed together and couldn't get enough of each other. On too many nights, they'd fallen into bed and merely slept.

After five years of marriage, she supposed it was natural for other parts of their life to take precedence, but she missed those small, sweet intimacies. She longed for his attention—the full measure of his devotion.

Right now, she felt that warmth. She saw it in his

gaze, heard it in his voice. It was as if they were falling in love all over again.

At the rental-car desk, Dylan used his fake I.D. to confirm the SUV that Carolyn had arranged for them.

Nicole didn't bother vamping it up for the clerk who she'd probably never see again. Instead, she went to a newsstand to grab a couple of energy bars, which seemed to be the only thing she could keep down. Her gaze lit on a stack of newspapers, including the *Vail Daily*. The front page headline screamed—Million-Dollar Ransom. *Oh, crap.*

Her fingers tensed as she picked up the paper. Her golden mood began to tarnish as she stared at the front-page photograph of Carolyn talking to the media and looking very authoritative. On an inside page were old photos of Dylan and herself. Apparently, their disguises were necessary.

She returned to the rental-car counter and laid the paper on the desk where Dylan could see it.

The clerk glanced over and said, "Isn't that something? That poor woman was held hostage for almost a week. I can't imagine what she went through."

Nicole's heart sank. The clerk's response mirrored her deepest fear: To be looked upon with pity. *I'm not a victim, dammit.*

"But she's all right now," Dylan growled.

"That's what they're saying." The clerk gave him a smile and the keys to their rental car.

Nicole followed silently behind him, shuffling along in her fancy cowboy boots and hoping nobody would notice her. She felt defeated. Nate had stolen her self-respect and made her feel powerless, helpless.

"Something wrong?" Dylan asked.

"I'm a marked woman. It's just a matter of time before everyone knows who I am. And what happened to me."

"Nobody has to know."

"I can't hide forever."

"Darlin', you've got nothing to hide."

*Except that I was a big coward. Terrified. Overwhelmed by my own filth. Ready to beg for a morsel of food.*

Dylan thought she was brave and strong. What would he think of her if she told him the truth? For now, she'd say nothing. Push the pain aside. Concentrate on the baby instead. She was pregnant, and that was exactly what she wanted. That was why she'd changed her mind about taking this trip. Her survival—her baby's survival—was all that mattered.

"I'm fine," she said.

"I know you are." His grin melted her heart. "Like I said to that clerk, you went through hell, but you're all right now."

Holding her head high, she firmly clasped his hand. In her mind, she echoed his words: *I'm all right now.*

She kept repeating that mantra while they drove the twenty-five miles to Glenwood Springs. On I-70, a steady stream of headlights cut through the night, but most of the traffic was headed east toward Denver—the skiers headed home after the weekend.

She turned on the overhead light to apply a thick gloss of lipstick and heavy kohl eyeliner. Digging through her purse to find her hairbrush, her fingers touched her cell phone. It was after six o'clock, she'd promised to call Nate. If she didn't make that contact, there could be trouble.

But she couldn't think about that now. She was safe. Nate didn't know where she was. There was no way—absolutely no way—he could find her. Her baby was safe.

Using her brush, she started teasing her hair—a ritual she only vaguely remembered from slumber parties when all the girls were trying to look like rock stars. She pushed her blond hair into a lop-sided shape. *Should have brought hairspray.*

"Interesting hairdo," Dylan said.

"I'm doing the best I can. I don't want to be recognized. I don't want to be 'that poor woman who was kidnapped.'"

"You're not that woman. You're Nicole Carlisle. Smart, independent and tough as hell." He took his eyes off the road to look toward her. "And beautiful."

"Even dressed like a tramp? With my hair sticking out like a porcupine?"

"Even so."

She sank back against the seat. "You don't know the half of what happened to me."

"Then tell me." His baritone dropped to a level that meant he was serious. "I don't want secrets standing between us."

*I can't go on like this.* The lies were a poison inside her, an infection that would fester and grow. She had to clean out her system for the sake of her baby.

"Later," she promised. "We'll talk later."

## Chapter Fourteen

Her usually reticent cowboy husband was so friendly and upbeat that Nicole was beginning to think he should always be disguised as Johnny Hellman. The frequent butt-patting and cleavage-ogling was a bit annoying, but otherwise Dylan was adorable. While picking up the key to the condo from the downstairs manager, he'd made jokes and chatted.

The three-story rectangular building had only nine units—three on each floor—and was perched on the hillside above the lodge. The wood siding and gingerbread trim on the balconies and along the eaves harkened back to the pseudo-Victorian design that was popular in many of the mountain towns, but these condos were far more modern. Though only three floors, the building had a huge elevator—big enough for several skiers and their equipment.

Dylan paused outside their room after fitting the key into the lock. He leered at her through his black-framed glasses.

"What?" she asked. "Is there something I should—"

He pushed open the door, turned and lifted her off her

feet. A totally unexpected move. She let out a shriek. "What are you doing?"

"Carrying my lady over the threshold." He swept her past the kitchenette into the front room and set her gently on the sofa. "Like a second honeymoon."

"Yes, dear. If we don't count the trashy disguise and the fact that a homicidal crazy man is after us."

"Nate will never find us here."

As he returned to the hallway to retrieve their bags, she sent up a quick prayer that he was right. Of course, he was. Nobody could know they were in Glenwood. The chopper had taken a crazy route. They were using different names. And this condo was far off the beaten path.

He returned to the sofa and dove on top of her. "How about it, Frankie? Ready for some action?"

"Tempted." But too many deceptions stood in the way of true intimacy. Before they made love, they needed to talk. "What about dinner?"

"For a sexy mistress, you're pretty damned practical."

"You know how it is with us gold diggers. Always keeping an eye on the bottom line."

"What does that mean?"

"You get no action unless you pay for it," she said as she climbed out from under him and stood. "Lobster and steak?"

He took off his glasses, shaking off the persona. "I want to avoid public places, like restaurants."

She circled the front room, an attractively furnished space with sliding-glass doors that opened onto a balcony. There was a built-in electric fireplace, a TV, a long table with benches and three sofas—all of which probably folded out into beds. This condo was designed for a family on a mountain vacation with one actual bedroom and a lot of other space for sleeping. In the kitchenette, she opened a cabinet over the microwave. "Not much here but salt, pepper and sugar. I guess we should stock up at the grocery store."

"It's only a little after eight," he said, checking his wristwatch. "Put on your bathing suit."

"Isn't the vest revealing enough?"

"After we stop at the market, we can go to the pool." He headed toward the door. "Which reminds me. I should have gotten the pass key that lets us into the pool area. I'll check with the manager and be right back."

When the door closed behind Dylan, Nicole exhaled a breath she hadn't been aware of holding. Maintaining her self-control took more effort than she realized. She wished she could wipe her memory clean and erase every trace of Nate Miller, but it wasn't possible. He was there inside her head. The only way to get him out was to tell all.

Thinking of Nate, she took her cell phone from her purse. There was one text message: Call. Or else.

She had to respond. Nate was capable of inflicting all sorts of mayhem on the people she loved.

Cell phone in hand, she opened the sliding-glass door and stepped outside, hoping for good reception. With the sleeve of her fringed jacket, she brushed a few inches of snow from the flat railing on the waist-high, fancy cut-out fence that enclosed the balcony. She looked down at the mineral-springs pool down the slope and to the left. Though Dylan had told her that it was huge, she was amazed by the size of the long, blue reservoir lit by lights below the water and swirling with the steam caused by ninety-degree water hitting the cold night air. Very impressive.

Beyond the Lodge and the pool was the highway. On the other side of the Roaring Fork River, the lights of Glenwood Springs glittered. The business section of town was brighter than usual with Christmas lights strung from the shops and trees. Though she couldn't make out details from this far away, she expected the town to be quaint and truly historical. Unlike some of the pre-fab, manufactured "Old West" towns, Glenwood was the real thing.

She decided to call Nate and get it over with. She punched in his number and reminded herself to sound as though she was sick in bed. Maybe she could channel the spirit of the consumptive Doc Holliday—gunslinger, dentist and tuberculosis victim—who Dylan had told her was buried here.

"You caught me just in time," he whispered. "I was deciding if I should shoot one of the ranch hands guarding the front gate or one of the horses."

"Don't shoot anyone," she moaned into the phone. "I'll do what you want. I've been too sick to move."

If he'd been monitoring the GPS device he'd left for her, he'd think she hadn't moved from the bed.

"Did you stop taking the sedatives?" he demanded.

"Yes, but I'm weak. So weak."

The sound of a train whistle cut through the night. Across the Roaring Fork, she saw the lights of a train. It whistled again.

"What was that?" Nate demanded.

"It's the TV," she said quickly. "I'll turn it down."

"Where are you?"

In those three small words, she heard rage and the threat of violence.

"In bed. Too sick to move."

"Don't lie to me, Nicole."

Panic raced through her. Real terror tinged her voice. "I wouldn't dare."

The phone went dead in her hand.

The train whistle sounded again.

Her fist clenched protectively in front of her belly. Nate still wouldn't know where they were. Railroad tracks criss-crossed the state. Unfortunately, none were close enough to the Carlisle ranch to hear the whistle blow there.

Frantic, she hit the redial button. It rang and rang. "Pick up, damn you. Answer me."

Nate's voice roared in her ear. "Tell your damn husband I'm coming for him."

"I'm sorry." Her heart pounded furiously in her rib cage. "I'll do whatever you want. Just promise me that you won't hurt anyone else."

"Call me in the morning."

He was gone again.

Shivering, she stared down at the glittering little town. Her vision blurred. Fear made her lightheaded. She had to tell Dylan about this new threat. Somehow, she would have to explain why she'd been in contact with the man who wanted to kill him. The man who'd said he'd kill one of the ranch hands or shoot one of the horses.

From inside the condo, she heard the door open.

Dylan came onto the balcony beside her. His arms wrapped around her. "You're shivering, darlin'."

"Cold," she said. And terrified to her core.

IT HAD TAKEN some coaxing for Dylan to convince his wife that they needed to leave the condo. Their ride in the helicopter had been the high point of the day—literally, and in every other way. After that, Nicole had been bummed by the clerk's comment in the terminal. Now, she was dark. Quiet. Edgy.

How was he supposed to woo this woman? The traditional courtship rituals, like chocolate and flowers, sure as hell weren't going to make a dent in her depressed mood. The whole time they were in the grocery store, he could barely get her to smile.

He needed patience, but it wasn't his nature to sit back and wait. He had one more plan for tonight. And it was a good one.

He parked their rental vehicle outside the gate leading into the pool. "We're going for a swim in the world's largest bathtub."

"Not tonight."

"You're already wearing your bathing suit. And I bought towels at the grocery store." He took the keys from the ignition and opened his car door. "Last one in is a rotten—"

"Stop it! I'm not playing around. We need to talk, and it's serious."

*Everything is serious with her.* Couldn't she take a break? Just be grateful that she'd survived? He slammed his car door and stood, looking up. On a clear winter night like this, the stars sparkled like diamonds. She needed to see these skies.

He circled the car, opened her door and held out his hand. "Come with me."

The heavy makeup she'd applied around her eyes had smeared. When she glared at him, she resembled a cranky raccoon. "Where are we going?"

"Swimming."

Slowly, with exaggerated reluctance, she placed her small hand in his.

He escorted her to the gate which opened easily with the pass key. The snow had already melted along the paved pathway that led to the red sandstone bathhouse where they could strip down, rinse off and leave their clothes in a locker. Wisps of steam rolled across the blue waters of the pool beside them.

He changed fast and waited for her outside the ladies' locker room. When she reappeared, barefooted, with a beach towel covering her blue bathing suit, he caught her hand and pulled her toward the shallow end. "The water's warmer down here."

"Only warm? You said it'd be hot," she grumbled. "How can they heat this thing? It's huge."

"Four hundred feet long, about a hundred feet wide."

Only a few people were in the pool. Through the clouds of steam and the vast expanse of water, the others were barely noticeable. He unwrapped her towel. The bruises on her forearms had already started to fade, but the sight of the injuries she'd suffered at Nate's hands sent a spurt of anger through him.

"You first," she said.

"Gladly." He slipped into the warm, soothing waters and held out his arms for her.

First, she sat on the edge. When her slender feet touched the water, she looked surprised. "It's warm."

"Well, yeah." Hadn't he told her about a hundred times? "That's why they call them hot springs."

She slid into the pool, into his arms for a quick hug. This area was only about three feet deep, and she bobbed once before submerging. When she bounced up beside him, the tangles in her hair flattened smoothly against her skull. She rubbed at her eyes, erasing the last traces of makeup. "It doesn't smell like chlorine."

"They installed an advanced filtration system." He didn't know the details. "This water is pure."

She pushed through the water with a breast stroke. Her slender legs trailed behind her in a pale reflection. He glided along beside her. The liquid warmth buoyed him, soothed him. He couldn't for the life of him think of why they hadn't come here before. Too busy to take a simple vacation? It seemed a poor excuse.

She disappeared under the water, and he ducked down to watch her undulate toward him. They locked lips and rose with rivulets streaming from them. He held her close, and her body molded against him. In the water, her familiar curves felt exotic and different. Her legs tangled with his.

Still kissing, he rolled to his back and pulled her with him through the water. She clung to him. Her breasts rubbed against his bare chest.

"Nice," she whispered. "Feels good."

"You feel good."

Underwater, he cupped her butt and fitted her against his erection. He was ready to make love, here and now. Probably not a good idea in a public place. They were supposed to maintain a low profile.

From the other parts of the pool, they heard the shouts of people running. Then there was the quiet of the night.

She separated from him, glided into deeper water and turned. "It's time for me to tell you a few things."

Her voice was so soft, he could barely hear her. "I'm listening."

"The first place Nate held me captive, that little room under Fiona Grant's barn, wasn't uncomfortable. There was a decent bed, and he left plenty of food and water. I was scared, but I felt strong and in control."

When he eased toward her through the water, she moved away, keeping a distance between them.

She continued, "I've been wondering. Why would anybody build a little room under a barn?"

"Nate built it himself. Before Fiona moved up here full-time, she paid Nate's ex-wife to stay at her house to keep an eye on things. She also hired Nate to do some handyman work, and he constructed that little nest so he could be close to his son."

Nicole ducked down so only her head was showing. Her eyes were more blue than the water. "That's sad."

"Sick," Dylan corrected her. "He was stalking his ex-wife. The poor woman had to take out restraining orders to keep him away from her and the boy."

"Her name is Belinda, right?"

"And her son is Mickey. He's the same age as Fiona's daughter. Those two kids helped find that hidden room. When I saw it, I couldn't believe you were there. We were searching every place, and you were so damn close."

"While Nate held me there, he brought water so I could wash myself. And a change of clothes."

"I know."

"How?"

"The proof-of-life pictures and videos." He'd stared at those tapes until his eyes were raw. At the time, he'd thought it might the last time he would ever see his wife. "The clothes he gave you once belonged to Belinda. That's how we finally figured out Nate was the one who kidnapped you. Belinda saw the tapes and identified her old clothes."

"I guess I owe her."

"We all do."

She paddled away from him. Though he knew it

would be good for her to tell the whole story of her kidnapping, he wasn't sure he wanted to hear what she said. At the moment, he had a grip on his hatred for Nate Miller. Dylan didn't think about killing that bastard more than once or twice a day. He couldn't afford to let his rage get the better of him.

He rose up from the water. "Let's soak in the therapy pool. It's even hotter than this one."

When they emerged from the water and the cold air hit their skin, they shivered together. In a few quick strides, they crossed the pavement to the therapy pool, which was heated to over a hundred degrees and was about a hundred feet long.

Dylan eased into the water with Nicole beside him. No one else was in sight. He settled into a comfortable position and allowed the heat to soak into his body. She leaned her back against him with her head resting against his shoulder.

"Hold on to me," she said. "This feels so good that I might fall asleep."

"I won't let you go." He kissed the top of her head.

"I'm afraid…" Her voice trailed off on a sigh. "If I tell you everything, I'm afraid you'll think less of me."

"I love you, darlin'." He tightened his grasp around her waist. "Nothing's going to change that."

"Even if I was a coward?"

"I should have been there to protect you." If anyone had cause for shame, it was him.

## Chapter Fifteen

Nicole nestled against Dylan's chest, and the steamy water of the mineral-springs pool caressed them both. The heat seeped into her muscles, soothing her aches and pains. Her bruised body was healing far more easily than her mind.

She had to let these terrible memories go. The longer she kept them bottled inside, the more they festered. The only way to release the pressure was to cut it open, like lancing a boil. And she knew it was going to hurt.

What she didn't know was how her husband would react. Would he hate her for being weak? With a sigh, she started speaking. "After I met you in the forest and told you… You remember what I told you."

"You hated my guts, wanted a divorce, blah, blah, blah." He gave her a little squeeze. "I never should have believed you."

"It's a good thing you did. If you'd made a wrong move, we both would have been shot."

"Are you saying I did the right thing?"

His breath whispered in her ear, sending a sensual message that she longed to respond to. Making love would have been sweet and satisfying, but until she told him—told him *everything*—it would be deceitful to take him into her bed. "I'd like to say that you always do the right thing."

"So would I," he said. "Keep talking."

"They threw me in the trunk of the car. Tied my wrists and ankles and slapped duct tape over my mouth."

When she said it aloud, the torture didn't seem so bad. But it was. "I tried to bite through the tape. My lips were chapped and the tape pulled against them. Tasted disgusting. The inside of my mouth was like glue, and I couldn't breathe. My nose closed up. I struggled. Banged against the trunk. Kicked as hard as I could. It felt like I was suffocating. Couldn't get air. I passed out."

She gulped down a huge breath of air to remind herself that she was free. "I thought I was going to die."

"Nicole, darlin', I wish—"

"Don't say anything." She slipped away from him. "I need to get it all out. If I don't, I'll never sleep easy again. I'll never recover." And she had to get better. For the baby. She needed to be strong.

"I understand."

His pale green eyes glowed. The light from the pool cast moist shadows below his high cheekbones and firm jaw. His shoulders were so wide, so strong. Even if they hadn't been married, she would have been drawn toward him.

She sank lower into the heated water—as cozy as a womb. She was ready to be reborn. "After being in the trunk of the car, I longed for that little room under Fiona Grant's barn where I was warm and had enough food. When he yanked me out and dragged me into his house in Riverton, Nate told me that he had the ransom, and there was no reason to keep me looking presentable. No reason to keep me alive."

"Why did he?"

"It's not me he hates, Dylan. It's you." She'd had plenty of time to think about this. "I was just his pawn. By not killing me, he kept his options open. He was trying to figure out how he could exact the most horrendous revenge against you."

She'd been totally aware of her unimportance. If she'd caused too much trouble, Nate would have murdered her without a qualm. She was nothing to him. She had to obey.

"In Riverton, he kept me locked up in a closet. I had duct tape on my mouth. Padded handcuffs on my wrists which were fastened behind my back. More duct tape around my ankles."

The memory took vivid shape in her mind. She recalled the intense discomfort. "My muscles ached. Under the duct tape, my skin chafed, itched something awful. When I cried, I couldn't breathe. But that wasn't the worst part."

Shame caused her to look away from him. "It wasn't the thirst when he refused to give me water. It wasn't the hunger. It wasn't the way he followed me to the bathroom and waited in the doorway for me to relieve myself."

In the water, she curled into a fetal position. "All those things were humiliating. I was filthy, ripe with sweat. And I felt like…" Words failed her. Explaining her emotional state was difficult. "Desperate and hopeless at the same time. I wanted to live. And I wanted to die."

"Never," he said. "Never wish for death."

His hand grazed her arm, but she slid away from him, gliding through the water. She couldn't bear for him to touch her until she'd gotten through this.

"The way I felt," she said, "reminded me of something that happened before we were married, back when I was working at Maud's clinic in Delta. We got a report of a dog that was being abused. It's not a vet's responsibility to investigate animal cruelty, but Maud has a big heart. She was determined to rescue the animal."

"And I bet you were, too."

"I was," she admitted. "We took the sheriff and went to a rundown house where an old man—his name was Wray—lived alone. A miserable old drunk. As soon as he saw us, he started yelling like a crazy person. The sheriff informed him that there had been complaints from neighbors about his dog."

They found the animal—a brown-and-black beagle mix with sad, rheumy eyes—chained to a clothesline without water or food. One of his ears was torn. Open sores on the dog's body had gone untreated and were infected.

"When I saw what Wray had done to his pet, I could have killed him. Anyone with an ounce of decency would have felt the same way. There must be a special place in Hell reserved for those who abuse a helpless creature. The sheriff told this jerk—this monster—that Maud and I would be treating the dog and sending him the bill."

She couldn't believe what had happened next. "As soon as we unfastened the chain, the dog staggered toward Wray. His tail wagging, he looked up at this man who had treated him so badly. I can't say it was love, but the dog knew that his survival depended on his master."

That described how she'd felt as a captive. "I looked to Nate. No matter what he did to me, I knew that I had to keep him happy. I had to do what he said."

Dylan came closer. "It's over now. You're free of him."

"Am I?" She ducked under the steam. Her tears mingled with the water of the pool. When she dared to look at her husband, she saw understanding in his gaze. "You don't think I'm a coward for not fighting back?"

"He could have killed you."

"I know, but—"

"Bravery comes in all kinds of packages. You chose survival. That took courage." He opened his arms. "Let me hold you, darlin'."

"Not yet." There was one more thing she had to tell him. "If I don't do what Nate says, I know that he'll hurt the people I love. Like the vandalism at Maud's."

"Nothing that he does is your fault."

Rationally, she knew he was correct. But that wasn't how she felt. "I have to obey him. Even now."

"Now? What do you mean?"

She heard a note of anger in his voice. *I don't want to tell him.* But she had to confess. She couldn't keep this secret anymore. "I've been talking to Nate. That's why I wanted the cell phone. When I went outside the house to the burned stable, I was following Nate's instruction. He left a GPS tracking device for me, and told me I had to keep it with me."

"Is it with you now?"

"No."

"Did you tell Nate where we were staying?"

She shook her head. "I've been telling him that I'm sick in bed and can't move. The GPS tracker is behind the bedside table at the house."

The faint lines across his forehead deepened. His mouth pulled into a straight, tight line. She knew that expression. He was thinking, running various options in his head.

The pale green of his eyes caught the reflected light from the waters. A muscle twitched in his jaw. Otherwise, he was as still as a rock. And silent.

"I'm sorry Dylan."

Her apology felt insufficient. She'd lied to him, betrayed the most basic, essential element of a good relationship.

"Why?" he demanded.

"I was afraid. Afraid for myself. And for you. Don't you see? I had to protect you."

Abruptly he stood, waist-deep in the steaming pool. Liquid spilled from his shoulders and down his muscular chest in a glistening stream. Powerful and strong, he strode toward her. He grasped her upper arms and lifted her through the water. His face was only inches away from hers.

"You've been through hell." His deep, quiet voice penetrated her fears. "I'm glad you told me about your captivity. I understand how much you were abused and hurt. Nate twisted your perceptions. But he didn't break you, Nicole. And he didn't break us."

"Can you forgive me?"

"I'm working on it." He kissed her gently. "When you decided not to tell me about your contact with Nate, you put yourself at risk. That's hard to forget. I never want to lose you."

"I'm not going anywhere."

"No more secrets."

She leaned against him and arched her neck, welcoming a deeper, more satisfying kiss. A familiar intimacy twined them closer together. Their marriage would survive; they were unbreakable.

There was one more secret. A happy surprise. She would save the news of her pregnancy for the perfect moment.

BACK IN THE BEDROOM of their condo, Dylan contacted Burke. On speaker phone so Nicole and Carolyn could participate, they started setting out the wide parameters of a plan to trap Nate.

Tomorrow morning, when Nicole called Nate, she'd arrange a meeting. Most important, she'd name the place.

"He'll never agree to that," Nicole said.

Over the speaker phone Burke said, "You need to make him think it's his idea."

"How can I do that?"

She sat in the center of the bed in her pink plaid flannel pajamas. Though the soothing waters of the mineral pool had eased some of the tension from her sore muscles, Dylan could tell she was still edgy from the way she fiddled with her hands and chewed her lower lip.

He thought of the duct tape slapped across her mouth, imagined her blue eyes wide with terror. A burst of rage exploded in the back of his head. *Hate* wasn't a strong enough word to describe the way he felt about Nate Miller. What had Nicole said about a special place in Hell?

Easing onto the bed beside her, he massaged the base of her neck. He sensed that there was something else going on with her—something she hadn't told him yet.

Burke—a trained negotiator for the FBI—gave Nicole some basic advice about how to deal with Nate. "Get him to agree with you. Ask him a question that he'll answer in the positive."

"Like what?" Nicole asked. "I have no idea what Nate wants."

"Me," Dylan said. "He wants my head on a silver platter. That's what you promise him."

She stared at him in horror and shock. "I could never do that. He won't believe me."

"You did a good job of play-acting when you told me you wanted a divorce," he reminded her. "This is pretty much the same thing."

"It's a place to start," Burke said. "Promise him that you'll deliver Dylan. Tell Nate that your husband is an insensitive pain in the butt, and you're sick of him."

"Hey!" Dylan objected.

"Truth hurts," Burke said.

"Just because I don't spill my guts every time I stub my toe—"

"Hah!" Carolyn interrupted him. His sister always had something to say. "I've know you since you were born, Dylan. You never express your feelings. I can count on one hand the number of times I've seen you cry."

That was how they were brought up. If his dad caught him whining, Dylan never would have heard the end of it. "Let's move on. Nicole tells Nate that she wants to dump me. Then what?"

"She names the place and the time. That's where we'll set a trap to catch him," Burke said. "Can you do it, Nicole?"

She reached over and caressed Dylan's cheek. "I'll try."

"We don't want to give him too much time to think about what you're saying. The quicker we pull him in, the quicker we can all relax."

Dylan looked down upon his wife's face, marveling that after all these years together, she was even prettier than when they'd first met. "We'll call you in the morning," he promised Burke. "Before Nicole contacts Nate."

"In the meantime," Burke said, "relax. You'll be safe in Glenwood. Nat doesn't know you're there."

Dylan disconnected the call. He held Nicole's face in his hands and studied her. "There's something else going on with you. Even an insensitive cowboy like me can see it."

"I talked to Nate tonight," she admitted. "When I was out on the balcony, I was talking to him."

"It's okay." Though he reassured her, he was a little bit irked. "What else?"

Her hands twisted into a knot on her lap. Sitting on the bed in her pajamas, she looked sweet and vulnerable.

"When I was talking to Nate, the train went through Glenwood. The whistle blew."

"And he heard it."

"I told him it was the television," she said.

Dylan sat back on his heels on the bed. If Nate believed her excuse, they were still safe. If not... "There are trains all over the state. He still doesn't know where we are. You didn't tell anybody else we were coming to Glenwood, did you?"

She shook her head. "Not even Maud."

"And Nate has to be monitoring that GPS tracker that's still at the house, right?"

"I'm sure he is." Her voice was tinged with bitterness. "With the tracker and the phone, he's still got me on his leash."

"Not anymore."

He took her hand and pulled her off the bed. He placed her in front of the mirror above the dresser.

"What are you doing?" she asked.

"Look at that woman in the mirror." He squared her shoulders. With his knuckle, he lifted her chin. "You're Nicole Carlisle. You survived seven days of captivity. You're strong and brave and smart. Do you see it?"

"Not really."

"That's a stubborn, determined little jaw. You're not going to let anything get in your way."

He stroked the line of her cheek. Her milky complexion contrasted with his rough hands. "You're like alabaster. Tough, strong and beautiful."

He leaned down so his face was right beside hers. His straight black hair pressed against her blond curls. "Look at us. We're different, but we belong together. What do you see in my eyes?"

"Your love."

"And that's never going to change."

"We'll get through this," she said. "I love you, Dylan."

# Chapter Sixteen

Nicole melted into his embrace. Right now, she didn't need sensitivity or analysis. She needed to be loved, and love was what her husband gave her. Steadfast and solid as a hill of boulders, he loved her. In spite of deception and fear, he still loved her.

"You're the best," she whispered.

He fitted her more closely against him. "About time you figured that out."

When she tilted back in his arms and gazed up at him, he started to trail kisses across her forehead. Then down to the tip of her nose. To her lips, where he lingered. Then he kissed along the line of her throat and lower, past her collarbone. When he reached the first button of her pajamas, he deftly unfastened it and nuzzled between her breasts. Another button unhooked. And another. A familiar warm thrill spread across her skin, and she felt herself beginning to blush.

Unlike her, he was fully dressed, except for his socks and cowboy boots. It didn't seem fair.

Her fingers latched on to his belt buckle. She pulled his shirt from his jeans. She'd bought this fancy cowboy shirt for him and had it tailored to fit snugly against his lean torso. She knew it fastened with pearl snaps. With one fierce yank, she tore the shirt open.

He did the same with her pajama top.

Bare from the waist up, they pressed against each other. Her tight nipples rubbed against the hair on his chest. A delicious sensation of flesh on flesh.

His voice rumbled in the back of his throat. A growl that never failed to arouse her.

"Take off your jeans," she demanded.

"Would that be the sensitive thing to do?"

"Do it. Before I rip them off with my teeth."

Laughing, he stripped them both at the same time. There was no need for game-playing. After five years of marriage, they'd seen each other naked plenty of times. Still, she paused to drink in the sight of him. His body amazed her. Long, lean muscles with a trace of dark hair, and a throbbing hard erection.

He lifted her off the floor to kiss her hard. Slowly, inch by inch, she slid down his body.

Turning her head, she glimpsed their embrace in the mirror. Her skin was whiter than his. His arm slung around her waist. His muscles were tight, chiseled. She realized that he was looking, too.

"We're good together," he said as he reached lower to cup her bottom.

"I wish I had more of a tan."

"Your skin glows. Like the pearls in that necklace Carolyn gave you last year."

"Last year for Christmas," she said.

He turned her so he could see her back side. "I love the way your waist dips in."

Turning her head, she checked out the rear view. "I might be too skinny."

"Darlin', you're perfect."

They kissed again. A long, languid kiss. Gradually, gently, they drifted onto the bed.

Dylan never rushed their lovemaking. Even when they were following a schedule in the hopes of getting pregnant, he made love thoroughly and deliberately. He nibbled at her earlobe, teased her nipples until she was writhing under his touch.

So desperately anxious was she to feel him inside her, she took charge, and straddled him.

He growled his approval as she slid onto him.

"Stay right there," he said.

His chest heaved as he stared up at her body, rising above him. His need surged up and met hers. They were joined in ferocious passion that grew more urgent with every thrust.

He flipped her onto her back. Spread her legs and drove hard. His strength overwhelmed her. It had been a while since they'd made love with such desperation. They'd been through a lot. They needed release.

She called out his name, wanting him deeper inside her, wanting to be joined with him. He was her husband, the man she adored. Her fine cowboy lover.

They poised together at the edge of climax, then fell onto the sheets, gasping.

Undulating waves of pleasure washed over her, reminding her of the sensual heat of the mineral spring pool.

"You're right," she said with a sigh. "We're very good together."

"The best."

Now might be the time to tell him that she was pregnant. Basking in the glow of incredible lovemaking, she felt that this might be the right moment. She cleared her throat. The magical words that would transform their lives were poised on the tip of her tongue.

But he spoke first. "This is the way our life is supposed to be." He leaned over and gave her a peck on the cheek. "In a world of our own. Just you and me."

"And our baby."

"Well, sure." He lay back on the pillows. "If it's in the cards for us to have a child, that's what will happen."

He didn't sound overjoyed about the prospect.

Resting her hand on her belly, she stared up at the ceiling. She didn't want to risk ruining this moment. It was better to wait.

THE NEXT MORNING Dylan slipped out of bed around five, leaving Nicole to sleep in. Her nightmares weren't completely gone. Last night when she'd jolted awake, he'd held her close, and she'd wept in his arms.

Though he never liked to see her cry, he knew those tears were part of the healing process. She needed to let out the pain. To talk about it. Cry about it. To scream and curse.

Whatever it took for her to get better, he'd be there for her. His love was stronger than ever. Making love to his wife was the best damn part of his life.

In the kitchen of the condo, he wished they were in a five-star hotel where he could call room service for steak and eggs. All he'd had to eat since they got here was a sandwich. He put on the coffee and dug around in the fridge. Maybe he should make her an omelet. Fluffy eggs with cheese on the top. Breakfast in bed would be romantic, and he needed to keep in mind his mother's advice about wooing Nicole.

But he was starving.

He grabbed a bowl of cereal and scarfed it down while the coffeemaker did its thing. With the edge taken off his hunger, he poured a mug of thick black coffee—nowhere near as good as the brew Polly made at the ranch—and went out on the balcony to watch the morning light extend across Glenwood Canyon. From this vantage point, he could see for miles—beyond the Lodge and the pool to the town across the Roaring Fork River. If he could see that far, it meant that anyone watching could also see him. He stepped back. He'd be a fool to start taking chances now.

Glenwood was at a higher elevation than the ranch, and there was a chill in the air. He pulled his robe more tightly around him. The skies were cloudy. Looked like snow.

But today might be a beautiful day. It might be the day Nate Miller was apprehended. Finally.

Though Dylan would never leave his wife unguarded, he wanted to be back at the ranch, setting up the ambush with Burke. He took out his cell phone and called.

Burke answered right away; he was already awake and planning strategy—probably sitting in the dining room, with Carolyn across the table, adding her opinions.

"We decided on the best place," Burke said. "When Nicole talks to Nate, she should tell him to meet her at the barn at the Circle M."

"Makes sense." Nate would feel comfortable coming back to his own ranch. "But he's not going to approach if he doesn't see Nicole and me standing there, waiting."

This part of the plan had bothered Dylan from the start. Nate wasn't going to be fooled by one of the ranch hands dressed up in a blond wig to look like Nicole.

"We've got the GPS tracker that Nicole left behind the bedside table," Burke said. "And I arranged for decoy FBI agents to come here and play the parts of you and Nicole."

Dylan didn't think it'd be hard to impersonate him, especially since he'd left his favorite hat back at the ranch. But no one was as pretty as Nicole. "What's going to prevent Nate from taking aim with his rifle and shooting these decoys from a distance?"

"We'll have enough surveillance to see his approach," Burke said. "Sharpshooters in strategic locations. As soon as he shows, we'll take him into custody."

Dylan trusted Burke when it came to planning logistical strategy. "What kind of timing are we talking about?"

"The earlier the better. Snow is predicted for the afternoon. If it's heavy, that could complicate things. Have Nicole make the call to Nate at nine o'clock. She should tell him to meet her at the Circle M at ten."

"Got it."

Dylan ended the call and went back inside.

Nicole was in the kitchen, sipping the coffee he'd made. Though she typically wore practical flannel nightclothes during the winter, she had on a black silky robe. When she came toward him, the robe gaped enough that he could see she had nothing underneath. Her hair was disheveled. Her cheeks, pink. A rush of appreciation went through him as she went up on tiptoe to give him a good-morning kiss.

"Your lips are cold," she said.

"I went outside so I wouldn't wake you."

"Who were you talking to?"

"Burke. He's got everything figured out. You should probably talk to him before you call Nate. At about nine o'clock."

A shiver twitched her slender shoulders. "I can't believe this is almost over."

"Would you like me to cook up some eggs? Serve you breakfast in bed?"

She raised an eyebrow. "You? Cooking?"

"I can do eggs."

"If we were out on the trail, using a skillet over an open fire, I'd defer to you," she said. "But this is a fully equipped kitchen. I'd rather do the cooking."

He rested his hand on the silky fabric at her waist. "Maybe we should go back to bed."

Her eyes shone with a sexy, sultry light. "Much as I enjoy being in bed with you, I'm a little tense."

"I could relax you." He nuzzled behind her ear.

"I'll bet you could," she purred. "And I could use something to calm me down. Later today, we can go to the hot springs caves. One of the brochures says they offer professional massage."

"I'm a pro," he said.

"Are not."

"As good as a pro. Something I picked up when I did bull riding at rodeos."

"I see." She trailed her finger along the line of his jaw. "Why is this the first I've heard about this talent?"

Whenever he mentioned rodeos, she gave him a lecture about how the animals were often mistreated. She had no sympathy for the cowboys who got bucked high and landed hard. Nicole hated those cattle prods.

He flexed his fingers. "Let me give you a rub-down."

For a few minutes more, she put up token resistance, dodging away from him and drawing him closer with her teasing. Then she succumbed to a long, deep kiss. As he'd known she would.

Their robes slid to the tile floor in the kitchen. Damn, he loved his wife.

A FEW HOURS LATER, Nicole sat at the table in the condo and stared down at the notes she'd made while Burke was giving her hints on how to handle her call to Nate. He'd told her to close her eyes and remember her fear so she'd still sound as though she was afraid of him. Not a pleasant prospect, but she was pretty sure she could convince Nate that she was willing to do his bidding. The harder part would be to sound believable when she denounced Dylan and offered to hand him over to Nate.

In real life, she'd never wish her husband harm. Even when she was furious at him, she wouldn't put him in danger.

Burke had advised her to be brief when she talked about her husband. The more she said, the more her real feelings would seep through.

She looked over at Dylan, who sat on the opposite side of the table. The taste of his kisses still lingered on her lips, even after a bacon-and-egg breakfast that she was managing to keep down in spite of her morning sickness. "I can't do this."

"You'll be fine," he said.

"Nate's never going to believe me. I'm not clever enough to convince him. I'm not an actress."

"Remember what Burke said." He rose from his chair. "When you tell Nate that you're sick of me, that's exactly what he wants to hear. He'll want to believe you."

"What if I can't pull it off?"

"Not a tragedy." He shrugged. "If Nate doesn't fall for our plan, we'll be no worse off than we are right now."

Except that Nate would be enraged. She feared his vengeance. "I'm scared."

"Darlin', I'm right here. I'll take care of you."

His hand went to the gun on his hip. When he'd got

dressed this morning, he'd fastened the holster and .22 on his belt. A more heavy-duty automatic rested on the kitchen counter. Dylan wasn't taking any chances.

"I'm not afraid for myself," she said. "But he'll go after the people I love. Not just vandalism like with Maud. He'll hurt them. Dylan, I don't think I can stand it. What if he shoots one of the horses?"

He leaned down and gave her a peck on the cheek. "I'm going to leave you here alone to make the call. That way, you can say whatever you need to say."

"Like what?"

"Like what a rotten bastard I am. How you can't wait to see me dead." He straightened his shoulders and flashed a killer grin. "Sounds seriously crazy when I say it out loud. A handsome cowboy like me? What sane person would want to hurt me?"

"We're not dealing with a sane person."

"You can handle him."

She watched him leave the room and close the door. She was alone with her cell phone—only a few rings away from her conversation with Nate. If she failed to convince him, it was going to be a problem. Burke had gotten the FBI involved, arranged for body armor and sharpshooters. It sounded as if he'd strategized for the invasion of a small country rather than setting up an ambush for one man.

At least she was being taken seriously. Everyone believed Nate was a threat. The dynamite he'd set to kill Dylan had probably gone a long way toward alerting them to the very real danger.

Might as well get it over with. She picked up the cell phone. Her palms were sweating as she punched in the number.

It was ringing. In her mind, she tried to practice her

complaints about Dylan. She had some real issues, like the way he never listened to her, didn't pay enough attention to her because he was too caught up in his work. But these petty problems sure as hell didn't merit a death sentence.

The phone kept ringing.

She had to make something up, something that would convince Nate that she despised Dylan. Abuse? She could lie and say that Dylan beat her. Or that he was messing around with another woman. That he had a mistress in Denver.

After twelve rings, Nate still hadn't answered.

*Maybe I called the wrong number.* She disconnected and dialed again.

The other-woman scenario seemed like the best bet, even though it was absurd to anyone who knew her husband. Dylan's middle name was loyalty. He wasn't the sort of man who messed around.

Again, no answer.

After getting all psyched up to make the call, she felt a huge let-down. What was Nate up to this time?

## Chapter Seventeen

Nicole tried to reach Nate again half an hour later. Then every fifteen minutes for an hour after that. Her nervousness about talking to him was replaced by a different brand of panic. *Fear of the unknown.*

"What's he doing?" She paced in front of the dining table in the condo. "He's out there." She jabbed emphatically toward the sliding-glass doors. "Out there. Somewhere. Wearing his black ski mask. Hiding in the shadows."

Dylan sat on the sofa, his long legs stretched out in front of him and his hands folded behind his head. His posture was typically laid-back. He appeared to be completely unperturbed and cool. He seldom showed emotion. Never let anyone see him sweat.

His attitude drove her crazy. "Dylan!"

"Yeah?" His lips barely moved when he talked. "What is it, sweetpea?"

This situation was shaping up to be a typical argument where she was hopping mad, literally shuffling from one foot to another, pacing and frantic. And he just sat there, as still and silent as a chiseled wooden sculpture of a cowboy.

"Aren't you worried?"

"Hell, yes." His eyes narrowed a fraction of an inch, which—in his case—indicated a massive show of emotion.

"How can you just sit there?"

"There's nothing I can do to make Nate answer his damn phone," he said with little inflection. He could have been reading a shopping list. "Things are going to work out."

"Will they?"

"Life goes on."

She stalked toward him, knelt on the sofa beside him and stared hard into his face. They'd come a long way in their relationship, and she wasn't about to backslide into old patterns. "I'm trying really hard not to explode like an atom bomb."

"And I do appreciate your restraint."

The irony in his voice irritated her. "Don't patronize me. Please. Don't."

Something in her voice must have sparked a realization, because he reacted. He lowered his arms and turned toward her. His gaze met hers directly. "You think I don't see what's going on here, but I do. I get it."

"Get what?"

"When you were kidnapped, I had time to think. Plenty of long painful hours when I regretted every dumb thing I've ever done." He paused. "Like now. I'm not handling this right."

"Don't blame yourself." They were in this dance together. "I'm at fault, too."

"Right before you got kidnapped, when we were talking in my office—"

"Arguing," she said.

"Arguing," he repeated her word. "You went storming off."

"Like I always do when I'm so mad I can't see straight. I needed to be by myself, needed time to settle down."

"And I didn't stop you," he said.

"How could you? When I get worked up, it's hard to—"

"Nicole," he interrupted her. "Don't make excuses for me. I should never have let you go. I've been doing this for years, taking the easy way out instead of stepping up and saying what I really mean. And what I feel inside."

"Your feelings?" She was stunned by this brand-new willingness to talk about what went on inside him. "Who are you, and what have you done with the insensitive lout I married?"

"I'm changing. Making a stab at it, anyway." He rose from the sofa. "When I say that things are going to work out, it's because I believe it. I believe in us. You and me and the love we have for each other. I believe that no matter what happens, we'll always come back to each other's arms. We'll always be looking toward the same horizon."

"I believe it, too."

"I like when everything is…normal. Peaceable. When there's no confrontation. A smooth, steady ride with no bumps in the road." He shrugged. "I never go looking for trouble. But sometimes it finds me."

She wasn't sure she liked the direction this was taking. "Are you talking about me? Am I a lot of trouble?"

"Yes, ma'am." He took her hand and pulled her off the sofa and into his arms. "But you're worth it."

He dropped a light kiss on her forehead, then continued, "The crazy part is that when I'm working, I expect problems. There's always something—from a lost little dogie to a drop in the market. And I work hard to set things right."

"I'll say."

Running the ranch sometimes meant being at his desk or in the saddle from sunrise to sunset. Dylan never shirked his responsibilities. There were days when she had to remind him to eat or drag him away from the desk at night to get some sleep.

"I guess," he said as he brushed a wisp of hair off her face and tucked it behind her ear, "that I need to work just as hard with you. To face up to our problems and deal with them, instead of trusting that everything will take care of itself."

She went up on tiptoe and kissed him. "That is the most romantic thing you've ever said to me."

"That's good. Because I don't think I'll ever be able to write you poetry."

"I bet you could." She gave him an encouraging nudge. "Go ahead."

He looked up at the ceiling for a minute, then back at her. "Here goes. Roses are red. Green is the grass. I like the look of your round, little—"

"Okay," she said. "Maybe you're not a poet."

"I could get into this," he teased. "What rhymes with *boobies*? Shoe trees? Two peas?"

With a laugh, she said, "That's enough, Shakespeare."

She hugged him because he'd lifted her spirits. But she stepped out of his embrace because she was still edgy. "We need to focus on the problem. Why isn't Nate picking up when I call?"

He sauntered toward the kitchen where he poured himself another mug of coffee. "It'd be good if Nate was more predictable. The timing is causing a problem for Burke and all the people he has ready for the ambush."

It was snowing at the ranch, a complication for their assault team. Burke had already told her to try to push her supposed meeting with Nate to tomorrow. "I'm surprised it's not snowing here. We're at a higher elevation."

"Colorado weather," he said, dismissively. "I was thinking about how you said he heard the train whistle blow when you were talking to him. Maybe he figured out where we are."

"How could he?"

"A person could figure out where a train is at a given point in time on-line. But that might be too high-tech for Nate."

"He did give me a GPS tracking device. Maybe he's getting smarter." She didn't really consider this dire possibility. "Even if he knew we were in Glenwood, he wouldn't know where we were staying. We're registered under fake names."

He nodded. "Or Nate might not be answering because he wants to mess with your head. Throw you off balance so you'll be more likely to give him what he wants."

"That sounds like something he'd do."

She pulled out a chair from the table and plunked down. With her elbows propped up, she stared at the clean, white wall of the condo. So much of her interaction with Nate had been game playing. He'd hold out a shred of hope, then snatch it away. He'd brought her water and clothing, made sure she was comfortable, then left her alone for a full twenty-four hours. Even though she knew his identity, he continued to wear a mask.

Dylan leaned down beside her and whispered in her ear. "You don't have to face him alone. I'm here."

And Nate didn't know that she and Dylan had mended fences, that their relationship was stronger than ever. For once, Nicole felt that she had the advantage.

She smiled up at her husband. "Before I made the first call to Nate this morning, I was thinking about ways I could convince him that I hated you enough to let him have his vengeance on you. I tried to think of you as an abuser or a guy who messed around with other women, and it was impossible. Completely, totally impossible."

"And?"

"You're a good man. A good husband. I've got nothing to complain about." She stroked his clean-shaven cheek. "Except for your poetry."

She picked up her cell phone again and put in another call to Nate.

This time he answered. "You're late. It's almost noon."

His voice shocked her into sudden alertness. She forced a fake cough, remembering to sound sick. "I tried earlier. You didn't answer."

"Make another mistake like that, and you'll be sorry."

She noticed that he'd dropped the whisper. His regular voice was just as ominous. "I'm ready to give you what you want."

"Why?"

"Because I can't live in fear anymore." That part was true, not playacting. "You want to come face-to-face with Dylan. And I can make that happen."

"I'm listening."

"We need to go over to the Circle M to check on the horses," she said. "It's snowing too hard today. But tomorrow. Ten o'clock in the morning. We'll be there. Just me and Dylan."

There was silence on the other end of the phone. Was Nate considering her offer? She closed her eyes, not daring to look at Dylan. She couldn't allow her voice to sound strong or triumphant. She needed Nate to think of her as his captive.

"And what do you expect to get out of this?"

"Your promise that you'll leave me alone." As if she could trust him? As if she'd believe him? "Please, Nate. I can't sleep. I keep throwing up. Please."

"Stop whining," he snarled. "I don't believe you. You wouldn't give up your precious husband."

"I don't want you to kill him. Oh, God, please don't do that. But the Carlisle family has hurt you. Maybe Dylan deserves a taste of your vengeance. He doesn't really understand what you've been through."

"What is he? A blind man?"

"What you really want from Dylan is an apology, right? You want him to ask for your forgiveness." She remembered how Burke had told her to get Nate to agree with her. "Isn't that right?"

"That would be a start."

"This is your chance." She really hoped he was buying this. "You can tell Dylan what's wrong with him and with all the Carlisles. Then you can take off."

"What?"

"You can walk away clean," she said. "Forget about the Carlisles. I know you kept a good chunk of the ransom money, enough to start a new life."

"Tomorrow," he said. "At the Circle M. Ten o'clock."

"Do we have a deal?"

"I'll think about it. You'll have my answer later today." He ended the call.

She opened her eyes and looked at Dylan. Even when

she was playacting, she couldn't throw him under the bus. But Nate didn't seem to mind. It had seemed as if he was considering her offer.

"This just might work," she mused.

DYLAN DIDN'T SHARE his wife's optimism.

Though he sure as hell didn't consider Nate Miller to be a mastermind, he knew the man to be cunning. Dedicated hatred fueled Nate's cleverness. All he wanted was revenge. Since he'd already defied the law and had little hope of evading charges for Nicole's kidnapping and the murder of Lucas Mann, Nate couldn't expect to get away clean. He had nothing to lose.

The more Dylan thought about the possibility that Nate had tracked their whereabouts using the train whistle, the more he believed they could be in imminent danger.

Nicole held a brochure in her hand. She smiled brightly at him. "These hot spring caves sound amazing. I think we should dress up like Frankie and Johnny and go there for a sauna and massage."

"You think they'd mind if I carry my gun?"

"Most people only wear a towel."

Much as he liked the idea of Nicole wrapped in a skimpy towel, getting all hot and sweaty, he said, "We're not safe."

She frowned. "Nate believed my story. He's going to hold off until tomorrow."

"Do you trust him?"

"No."

"Let's look at it another way," he said. "If Nate comes to Glenwood looking for us, he's got plenty of cash to bribe hotel clerks."

"Lucky for us, we're not staying in a hotel. He won't

find us." She waved the brochure. "This is a vacation destination. There are dozens of places to stay."

In this situation, the wealth of the Carlisles was a detriment. "Carolyn made our reservations. It doesn't take a genius to figure out that we're staying in a fairly high-end place. Right off the bat, Nate could eliminate ninety percent of the motels."

She slapped the brochure down on the table. "What should we do?"

He picked up the automatic that was resting on the table beside the sofa and checked the clip. "Put this in your purse, grab your jacket and let's go."

"Back to the ranch?"

"Burke's got things under control there," he said. "I want to get you somewhere safe. Let's head for Denver. I can buy you some pearl earrings to match that necklace you got last Christmas."

"Christmas shopping?"

"You bet."

She gave a quick nod. "Give me a minute to pack my bags."

In his mind, he envisioned Nate creeping toward the condo, positioning himself to take a shot as soon as they showed themselves. Dylan needed to be able to move freely, didn't want to be burdened down with suitcases. "Leave the bags. I want to get on the road."

"I can't." She headed toward the bedroom. "There's something I can't leave behind."

He followed her. "What's so important?"

She flipped open the top to her larger suitcase. "Just something."

"What?"

She whirled to face him. "Lucas Mann's ashes."

## Chapter Eighteen

"That old son of a bitch is dead, and he's still causing me problems."

"Lucas was like family."

Nicole threw a couple more items in her suitcase and closed it. She had no intention of leaving behind the cardboard box containing the ashes of their late foreman. She'd brought his remains, thinking they might find the perfect place to scatter them. Maybe on the top of Mount Sopris. Or in the Roaring Fork River. In any case, Lucas was with them now, and she wouldn't leave him behind.

Dragging the suitcase, she staggered through the bedroom toward the door leading into the hallway.

With his gun in his hand, Dylan opened the door a crack and peeked outside. "Give me the damn suitcase and take the gun out of your purse."

She resisted. "I can carry Lucas."

"I've got it," he muttered. "I wondered why this suitcase was so heavy."

"The ashes only weigh nine or ten pounds."

"How the hell do you know that?"

"Looked it up on the Internet." She glanced back into the room. "Maybe I should grab the laptop."

"We're going," he said. "Now."

At the door leading from the condo building into the parking lot, Dylan paused again to scan. They ducked and ran, jumping into the car as quickly as possible.

As he turned the key in the ignition, Dylan glanced over his shoulder to the suitcase in the backseat. "Buckle up, Lucas. Wouldn't want you getting injured in an accident."

She peered through the windshield as Dylan drove onto the narrow, winding road leading down into town. A perfect place for an ambush. She realized that she was gripping the handle of the automatic with her finger on the trigger. Instead of putting it down, she prepared herself to shoot. Nate could be hiding amid the surrounding trees, waiting to pick his shot. He could shoot out a tire. Fire through the windshield.

Adrenaline rushed through her veins and jump-started her pulse. When they circled through town and finally merged onto the highway, she breathed a sigh of relief. They were on their way.

Though it was entirely possible—likely, even—that Nate was still back in Delta, she felt that they'd made the right decision. "We dodged that bullet."

"I could be overreacting," Dylan said. "But I'd rather be too careful than not careful enough. I almost lost you once. It's not going to happen again."

A light snow had started to fall, blurring the rugged landscape of rocks and trees. In the past couple of years, forest fires had taken their toll on the canyon, leaving much of the sloping hillsides barren.

The snowfall wasn't enough to seriously impede the traffic, and Dylan handled the SUV with easy expertise.

"I guess I can put the gun away," she said.

"For now," he said.

"Should I call Carolyn and tell her about our change in plans?"

"Not just yet. She and Burke have their hands full with preparations for the ambush. No point in second-guessing their operation. They might still need to put it into effect. Besides, we've got plenty of time to make that call."

Leaning back in the passenger seat, she turned her head and studied his strong profile. He wasn't wearing his usual cowboy hat, and his tousled black hair fell over his forehead. His gaze focused on the road ahead.

"Are you angry?" she asked. "Because I brought Lucas along?"

"It's kind of sweet. Crazy, but sweet. I can't really bring myself to hate the old man."

"Of course not. Not after all the years he worked at the ranch."

"It's hard for me to forgive him. But you're right, darlin'. The good times outweigh the bad."

Her taciturn husband was becoming a pro when it came to forgiveness. In so many ways, he was proving the depth of character that she'd always known he possessed. She felt closer to him by the minute.

They were almost to the Vail exit when the cell phone in her purse rang. She recognized the caller ID. "It's Nate. What should I tell him?"

"Pretend that you're still at the ranch."

She answered, "Hello?"

"Go to the front desk at the Mount Sopris Hotel in Glenwood Springs. There's a package waiting for Dylan Carlisle. Both of you need to be there."

Looking at Dylan, she repeated his words. "You want me and my husband to go to the Mount Sopris Hotel in Glenwood?"

"I made a reservation in your name."

"A reservation under the name of Carlisle?"

"Be there within the hour."

Anger burned through her. "How the hell can I be at that hotel in an hour? Check your GPS tracker. I'm at the ranch."

"I know where you are," he said. "In Glenwood."

"Not anymore." Dylan's instinct had been right. Nate had been on their trail, but they'd outsmarted him. "We're long gone."

"Turn around. Go to the Mount Sopris Hotel, pick up the package and wait for further instructions."

"Why the hell do you think I'd do as you say?"

"To save Maud."

"You kidnapped Maud?"

Stunned, she looked to Dylan for help. In a low voice, he said, "That's not possible. The sheriff was protecting her. Ask him for proof."

Into the phone, she said, "I don't believe you."

"Proof of life." She could hear the sneer in his voice. "That's supposed to be the first step in a kidnapping. Dylan learned his lessons well. But Maud can't talk right now. She's in the trunk of my car. You remember that, don't you? Being tied up and breathing in the exhaust fumes?"

A sob caught in her throat, but she had to be strong for Maud's sake. It wouldn't do any good to break down in tears, no matter how much she hated to think of her dear friend going through the same trials she had. "I want proof."

"Maud told me a couple of things. She lived in the town where you grew up in Wyoming—Rawlins. On your sixteenth birthday, a friend of yours hit a stray dog with his car. You took the dog to Maud and you worked together to save the animal."

She vividly recalled the incident. Saving that stray was one of the reasons Nicole decided to be a vet.

He continued, "Maud's middle name is Primrose."

Very few people knew that.

"When she was thirty-five," he said, "she was in a bad car accident and ended up having a hysterectomy. Want me to start describing her scars?"

Nicole was convinced. "Let me talk to her."

"In good time," he said. "Do what I told you first. And if you contact anybody, if I see one deputy sheriff, Maud's dead."

"Why would you kill her? She never did anything to—"

He had already disconnected the call.

DYLAN PULLED OFF the highway and parked on a side street. A few minutes ago, they'd been talking about Christmas shopping. Not anymore. Nate had turned the tables, and they'd lost every advantage.

"First thing," he said, "we'll do everything to make sure Maud isn't hurt."

Nicole blinked furiously, fighting back tears. "How do we know that he hasn't already…"

"That's not the way he works."

Dylan was on familiar ground—he'd already been through one kidnapping scenario with Nate. "Give me your phone."

"Why?"

"From now on, I'll do the talking. You don't have to go anywhere near that crazy son of a bitch. He's not getting his hands on you. Not again."

"I have to respond. It has to be both of us going into the hotel. He was specific." She rested her hand on her belly and winced, and hoped she wasn't going to throw up again. "If I don't do what he says, Maud will suffer."

"He's not after Maud. Or you." This much, Dylan knew for sure. "Right now, I'm his target. He wants his revenge against me."

"Do you expect me to sit back and let you walk into danger?"

"I could ask you the same question."

"We don't have time to argue," she said. "We have to be at the hotel in an hour."

"Fine," he started the engine. "We can argue while I drive."

Circling around, he got back on the highway. His jaw was clenched tight. His mind raced. He had to find a way to keep Nicole safe. If it came to a showdown between him and Nate, that was okay. Dylan could handle himself.

"We can't contact the police," she said.

"Agreed."

"And I'm coming into the hotel with you. Understand?"

In a way, he did understand. When she'd been kidnapped, he would have given his right arm to be with her. Or to trade places with her.

"Dylan? Talk to me."

"I've got nothing to say."

"You promised you wouldn't pull the strong, silent routine! I know there's something going on inside your head. You've got to let me in." Through her anger, he heard a pleading note. "What are you thinking? Please, tell me."

"I don't have a plan," he said. "All I know is that this time, I need to be smarter. To think one step ahead of Nate."

He took his cell phone from his pocket.

"What are you doing?" she asked. "We can't contact anybody. He'll hurt Maud."

"I'm not calling the sheriff." Sheriff Trainer had already proven himself to be incapable of protecting Maud. "But I'm not following Nate's rules. We need backup. I don't know how bad the snow is at the ranch, but I'm guessing this isn't good timing for a chopper flight. I want to get Jesse and Burke on the road."

"Bad idea."

"You haven't had a chance to see those two guys in action." Burke knew the ins and outs of negotiating. He was smart and capable of arranging a complex rescue. Jesse had to be the best damn tracker Dylan had ever seen in action. Plus, he was a sharpshooter. "I'm calling."

She shook her head. "If Nate sees them, he'll hurt Maud."

"The last time I dealt with Nate, here's what happened. He set up two points of contact in two different directions. I went one way and met with you. Carolyn delivered the ransom."

That arrangement had worked successfully for Nate. There seemed to be no reason for him to change his tactic. "He'll probably do something like that again. Send us off in different directions."

"He can't do that again. He doesn't have two other people to watch the second position."

But he had plenty of money for a hired gun. And Nate was playing with dynamite now. There were plenty of ways he could rig a second location. "We need to be prepared. I trust Burke and Jesse to stay out of sight."

He made the call, emphasizing to Burke that they

needed to lay low. If Nate spotted them, there was no telling how he'd react.

"The roads are bad," Burke said, "but we'll be there as quickly as we can."

Dylan stared through the windshield as he continued to drive. The exit for Glenwood Springs was only a few miles ahead. "I hope we don't run into any problem at the hotel."

"Park as close to the entrance as you can," Burke advised. "Have your gun ready. Once you get inside, it doesn't seem likely that he'd shoot you in the hotel lobby."

Dylan agreed. "He said he left a package for me."

"Could be instructions for what he wants you to do. Hang in there, Dylan."

"There's something I need for you to do," he said.

"Anything."

"Bring my hat."

"You got it, cowboy."

He exited the highway. Snow had begun to accumulate on the wreaths and evergreen boughs decorating the streetlights on the main road. The old-fashioned storefronts in Glenwood Springs looked as pretty as a Christmas card. At a stoplight, Dylan scanned the faces of the few pedestrians on the sidewalks. Nate wouldn't stand out in a crowd. He was average height and weight, probably dressed in typical western wear.

Dylan drove past the Mount Sopris Hotel, a historic building. Made of sandstone and five stories high, the hotel had been built in the early 1900s to accommodate tourists and those who came to the hot springs for their health.

"You're not stopping," Nicole said.

"We've got a little time before Nate's deadline." He

glanced toward her, concerned. After their brief disagreement, she'd been quiet, and that worried him. "Are you okay?"

"Been better." She forced a brave little smile. "Do you think he'll try anything when we're on the street?"

Though Dylan couldn't comprehend most of what was going in Nate's twisted mind, he had an answer for her. "I don't expect to get gunned down outside the hotel. Nate wants revenge, wants to make sure I suffer for all the wrongs he blames on my family. He wants to see my face before I die."

"Oh, hell."

"Come on, darlin'. That's good news. Better than winding up dead on the sidewalk."

She shuddered. "Do me a favor, Dylan. Don't reassure me with any more supposedly good news."

He could tell that she was getting some of her spirit back, and he was glad to see her spunky instead of scared. "We've still got time. I want to take you back to the condo, where you'll be safe. You can stay there until Burke and Jesse arrive."

"That's not going to happen."

"I don't want you putting yourself in danger."

"Well, that's too damn bad," she said. "Nate wanted both of us—you and me—to show up at the hotel, and I refuse to do anything that puts Maud in more danger."

"He's not going to hurt her. Without Maud, he loses all leverage."

"I won't take that chance." The determined edge in her voice told him further argument was futile. "I'm coming with you."

Reluctantly, he conceded. "Starting right now, I need you to do exactly what I say."

"Absolutely."

How the hell had this woman ever thought of herself as a coward? As far as he was concerned, she was too brave for her own good.

"When I park the car," he said, "wait for me to come around to your side and open the door. Keep the gun in your purse but within easy reach. We'll hustle inside fast. Are you with me so far?"

"Got it," she said. "Then what?"

"We'll go to the front desk. I'll pick up the package. I'm going to open it right there."

"Okay."

"Then we go up to our room."

She reached over and touched his arm. "I love you, Dylan."

"I know."

He pulled into a slot on the street in front of the hotel, parked and exited the car. There were too many places on the old-west street where a man with a rifle could hide. A shiver went down his spine as he imagined taking a bullet between the shoulder blades.

Dylan didn't think Nate would attack now. But he didn't know. He couldn't know. Nate Miller was pure evil.

When he opened Nicole's door, he shielded her with his body as he directed her into the hotel. Inside, it was quiet and warm with a faded Victorian charm that came from marble floors, potted green plants and fancy designs on the wallpaper. Two elderly women sat on a velvet sofa with claw legs. There was no one else in sight. He went directly to the long front counter of rich, polished wood.

"I'm Dylan Carlisle. You're holding a room for me."

"Yes, sir." The woman at the front desk found a key

and a package in a padded envelope. "The gentleman who made your reservations left this."

"That was no gentleman," Nicole muttered. "Did he say where we could reach him?"

"No, ma'am."

"Have you noticed him hanging around? Maybe waiting for us?"

"I haven't."

Dylan stared at the envelope with his name scrawled across the front. He'd heard about letter bombs, but didn't think Nate was clever enough to put one together. Gritting his teeth, he tore the envelope open.

Inside was a thick book with a worn, red leather cover.

Nicole touched the cover. "Maud's journal."

## Chapter Nineteen

With the book in her hands, Nicole stood outside the door to their room on the second floor. When Dylan gestured for her to step back against the wall, she immediately obeyed. Though she'd insisted on coming to the hotel, there was no power struggle here. Following his instructions reassured her; she trusted him to keep her safe…as safe as possible.

She peered down the narrow hallway, dimly lit with wall sconces above dark wainscoting. According to local legend, Mount Sopris Hotel was haunted, but she wasn't on the lookout for ghosts. Her ghost was real, solid and dangerous. Nate could appear at any second, stepping out from the stairwell, exiting the elevator and charging toward them. "Hurry, Dylan."

He twisted the old-fashioned key in the lock. His gun was in his hand, ready to shoot back if Nate was waiting for them in the room. Dylan slipped inside and immediately hit the lights. "Stay with me," he said.

Just inside the door to their room, she watched as he did a quick search of the room and adjoining bathroom. Compared to the condo with kitchenette where they'd been staying before, this bedroom was cramped and small. Apparently, Nate was too cheap to spring for a suite.

"Should I lock the door?" she asked.

He gave a quick nod. Passing the window, he pulled down the shade. His search deepened as he peered onto the upper shelf of the closet, opened all the drawers and looked under the bed. Finally, he holstered his gun. "That'll have to do."

"What were you looking for?"

"Nate used dynamite the last time I saw him."

"A bomb?" She hadn't considered that horrifying possibility. "I thought you said he'd want to kill you up close and personal."

"I'm trying to think of everything." His jaw tensed. "This set-up doesn't feel right."

She had to agree. Nate knew exactly where they were, and that knowledge gave him an edge.

She sat on the hardwood chair beside the small desk. The only other piece of furniture in the room was an armoire that held the television. She placed Maud's journal on the desk. It seemed wrong to read it. By definition, a journal was private. "Why would Nate leave this for us?"

"As proof that he has Maud."

"But it's not." She'd seen the red leather spine many times. The fading gilt letters spelling out *My Journal* had attracted her attention. "Maud kept the journal on the bookshelf at her office. Nate could have grabbed it when he ransacked the place."

"Take a look inside. There might be clues."

Feeling like a snoop, she opened the worn binding. The first entry—scribbled with rushed penmanship—was dated fifteen years ago. At that time, Maud had been in her early thirties. It read: "A fine place to set up my first veterinary practice. I'm going to like Rawlins, Wyoming."

Though Nicole didn't recall the date, she remembered when Maud had started introducing herself around town. Everybody liked the tall, skinny woman who dressed in bright colors, and they were glad to have a vet who took care of dogs and cats, as well as large animals.

The entries in the journal were sporadic and brief, following no particular pattern. Nicole easily imagined her friend sitting down when she had a chance and jotting down a sentence off the top of her head. The colors of ink varied, typical of Maud. There were remarks about her canine or feline patients that made Nicole smile.

On the third page was a slightly longer entry: "I spoke to Nicole for the first time today. Doesn't like to be called Nickie. A beautiful, intelligent girl. Blond like me. I thought she'd be taller."

"Taller than what?" Nicole mumbled. She scanned through a couple of pages, looking for her name. After that first entry, Maud referred to her as N.

One entry stood out. Written in purple ink, it said, "Tomorrow is N's birthday. She'll be fourteen. Should I tell her? She seems so happy with her mother and father. Good people. I don't have the right to disrupt her life."

Nicole looked up from the pages. When Dylan caught her gaze, he immediately came toward her and leaned down, looking into the pages of the journal. "What's wrong?"

"Maud was keeping some kind of secret from me. It was a long time ago, back when she first moved to Rawlins."

"Something important?"

"I don't know." But she felt apprehensive, as if standing at the edge of a precipice, knowing that if she took that last fatal step she could never turn back. "I'm not sure that I want to know."

"How bad could it be?" he asked.

"I've known Maud since I was…" She glanced at the pages. "Since I was fourteen. And I know her to be a kind, decent person. I've always thought of her as my mentor."

"And the secret?"

"I'm sure it's nothing bad."

She was closer to Maud than just about anybody else. When Nicole went off to college, Maud had moved to Delta and expanded her practice. She'd given Nicole her first job when she graduated. It was hard to believe that she'd been keeping a secret for all these years.

Nate had mentioned the incident with the stray on Nicole's sixteenth birthday. She flipped through the pages of the journal until she found the date. With Dylan looking over her shoulder, she read the entry: "I'm so proud of N. She handled herself like a champ in surgery. Said she wanted to be a vet. Like me! She's everything I dreamed of. My beautiful daughter."

*Daughter.* Maud's scratchy handwriting faded as Nicole's eyes filled with tears. *Maud is my birth mother.*

The news hit her like a stampede. She jumped to her feet. The inside of her head whirled like a tornado. Like most kids who were adopted, she'd wondered about her birth parents. But only occasionally. Nicole loved and respected the parents who'd raised her; she'd never felt the need to search for the woman who gave birth to her.

*Because she was nearby all the time.* From age fourteen until now, Maud had been watching over her.

"Why didn't she tell me?"

"Don't know."

"She was really young when she got pregnant. Maud's forty-six. And I'm twenty-nine." She did the math. "She was sixteen when she had me. And put me up for adoption."

"And you were placed in a good home," Dylan said. "I've never heard you say anything bad about your mom or dad."

"It wasn't perfect. We had our ups and downs, but they always supported me, encouraged me. They taught me the importance of family." The reality struck her. "I have a family again. I have a mother."

Even better, she had a mother who loved her. Maud was someone she could trust, someone she respected. She remembered the joy in Maud's expression when Nicole had announced that she was trying to have a baby. How would she feel when she knew she was going to be a grandmother?

Her mind reeled. What if she'd found her mother only to lose her again? "Oh my God, Dylan. How are we going to rescue her?"

His gaze was calm and steady. For once, she appreciated his rock-hard demeanor. "I'll make this right. First thing we're going to do is leave this room."

"But, we—"

"Nate didn't say anything about staying holed up in this hotel." He took her hand and pulled her toward the door. "Let's get out of here."

She balked. There should be no more secrets. "There's something I've got to tell you."

"Walk and talk at the same time."

She had to tell him about the pregnancy. There would be no more secrets. "This is important, really big."

"I'm sure it is." He opened the door. "We're going downstairs to have some lunch. I saw a dining room when we came in."

"What about Nate?"

"If he needs to contact you, he's got the phone number." He adjusted his jacket to hide his gun. "Bring the journal."

Though she was bursting with the need to tell him, Nicole held herself in check. This might not be the best time to drop another emotional bombshell.

They went down the stairs instead of taking the elevator. As they crossed the lobby, she tried to stay alert to her surroundings. If they ran into Nate, she needed to be ready to respond. It took every shred of her dwindling composure to merely place one foot in front of the other.

Maud's journal weighed heavily in her hand.

WHEN THEY WERE SEATED in the dining room, Dylan took a position with his back to the wall so he could watch the entrance to the restaurant. The fact that Maud was Nicole's birth mother was an added complication in an already tangled mess. *How the hell am I supposed to deal with all this?* He wasn't a trained federal agent like Burke. Or a bodyguard like Jesse.

He stared across the table toward his wife. The color had returned to her face, but her eyes were too bright. She looked feverish and a little bit panicked.

"I wish," he said quietly, "that I could do better. For you."

"What do you mean?"

"I don't know how to strategize in a hostage situation. I can't put together all the clues and figure out where Nate is hiding with Maud. I'm just a rancher."

She leaned across the table and rested her hand atop his. "I wouldn't have you any other way."

"Still… It might be handy if I was a trained commando."

"I fell in love with a cowboy," she said. "When the time comes, you always do the right thing."

"I sure as hell hope so."

"Now, maybe you can tell me why it was so important for us to leave our hotel room?"

"Nate was here before we arrived. He could have planted a bug in the room." If Dylan had been an experienced lawman, he might have been able to find a listening device. "I didn't want take a chance on having him overhear our plans."

"You have a plan?" She brightened.

"The only thing I can think of right now is to stall until Burke and Jesse get here."

He checked his wristwatch. It was less than two hours since he'd called Burke. Not nearly enough time for the reinforcements to get here.

They had ordered coffee as soon as they sat down. When the waitress brought it, Dylan asked her to leave the pot. The hotel restaurant seemed to be upscale for a tourist town. White cloths on the tables. Heavy silverware. Soft background music.

The waitress took a pad from the pocket of her clean white apron. "Are you ready to order?"

Dylan asked, "Where do you get your beef?"

"It's Carlisle Certified Organic, sir."

He grinned. Finally he'd found a bright spot in this otherwise dismal day. "I'll have a burger with everything. Medium rare and juicy."

"Same here," Nicole said.

As soon as the waitress left, Nicole warned him. "Don't tell her who we are. There are still reporters looking for us."

"Maybe some of them are armed," he joked. "I'm so desperate for backup that I'd even use a pencil-pusher with a gun."

"Swell idea." Her tone was brittle, but a tiny grin lifted the corner of her mouth. "Or we could get one of those TV cameramen to tape us. Have our own reality show."

"Carolyn would have to be the star."

"Oh, yeah." She chuckled. "Wouldn't your sister love that kind of exposure?"

Her laughter gave him hope. He didn't want her to be scared, didn't want Nate to have control over her. "Hold on to that smile. I'm going to check in with Burke."

Making phone contact with Burke was the biggest reason he didn't want to stay in their room. He couldn't take a chance on having Nate know that he and Nicole had backup.

As soon as Burke answered, Dylan filled him in on their whereabouts. "Where are you?"

"On the highway. The snow is slowing us down. But we ought to be there in an hour."

"The faster the better," Dylan said.

"We checked at Maud's house. No sign of a struggle, but she's nowhere around. Her office said she called in sick."

Dylan had been sure from the start that Nate wasn't lying about holding Maud captive. "Anything else?"

"Maud's car is gone."

Her van had heavy-duty all-terrain tires. The rear area would be a good place to hide a kidnap victim. "You think Nate took the van?"

"That'd be my guess," Burke said. "Have you got a plan for the next time he calls?"

"I was kind of hoping you'd come up with something."

"Same stuff I told Nicole before. When Nate calls, she needs to get proof of life. She should ask to talk to Maud. Tell her that she wants to make Nate think that you're going to cooperate. Let him believe that you'll do whatever he says. And stall."

Dylan ended the call with a promise to stay in touch, then he grinned at Nicole with a confidence he didn't really feel. "We're going to be all right."

"You're sure about that?"

"As long as I don't get thrown any more curveballs. I don't need anything more to worry about." He took a sip of coffee. "There was something you wanted to tell me before we left the room."

"It'll wait."

Her gaze slid away from his, and he knew she was hiding something. *What now?* "You're sure?"

"Absolutely." She tossed her head, and the light shimmered in her blond hair. "Did Burke have any other instructions?"

He ran through the list of negotiating tactics. Burke's suggestions weren't the way Dylan did business. He was accustomed to being direct and making an honest offer, laying his cards on the table. Sure, there would be some bargaining. But when he sealed the deal, both sides were clear about what was required. And when he gave his word, he followed through.

Their hamburgers came, and he was happy to just sit back and enjoy fine beef. It was something to be proud of.

Nicole's appetite had improved. He liked the way she made little happy noises when she ate.

"Mmm." She took a huge bite. "Oooh."

"Good," he said.

In a ladylike gesture, she dabbed at the corners of her mouth with the cloth napkin. "I didn't realize how hungry I was."

"Chow down. You're going to need to keep your energy up."

"Why's that?"

"Kicking Nate Miller's ass is going to take some effort."

"I like the way that sounds." She took a sip from her water glass. "Kicking ass."

The phone in her purse rang, and he checked his watch. If Burke and Jesse stayed on schedule, they should be here in half an hour.

She read the caller ID on the phone. "It's him."

The only person Nate had communicated with was Nicole. Burke would probably advise that she remain the contact person. They had some kind of rapport.

But Dylan was tired of playing by rules he didn't understand. He stuck out his hand. "Give me the phone."

# Chapter Twenty

Burke probably would have advised Dylan not to take Nate's call, but the relief on his wife's face told him he'd made the right decision. Without objection, she handed the ringing cell phone to him.

He answered, "This is Dylan Carlisle."

There was a pause. Then, Nate said, "Put Nicole on the phone."

"I'm the one you're after." At the sound of Nate's voice, rage shot through Dylan's veins. Every muscle in his body tensed. "Let's talk, Nate. You and me. Man to man."

"You brought this on yourself." Nate's hatred spewed through the phone. If words were bullets, they'd both be dead. "The high-and-mighty Carlisle family hurt a lot of people. You've got enemies."

He wouldn't argue that point. With power came adversaries. When Nicole was first kidnapped, they'd made a list of people with grudges. A very long list. But Dylan's conscience was clear; he had a deserved reputation for fairness. His ranch and associated businesses kept a lot of people employed. There were ten times more friends than foes.

"Put Maud on the phone," he said. "Before I make any kind of deal with you, I need to know she's all right."

"You're not the boss, Dylan. Don't make the mistake of thinking I'm one of your ranch hands. Some dumb cowpoke you can order around."

"I never thought you were stupid." Tamping down his anger, Dylan tried to follow Burke's instruction to establish a rapport. He might be able to play on his shared history with Nate. Though they'd never been friendly, they'd lived only five miles apart all their lives, attended the same schools, went to the same parties. "You were a couple of years ahead of me, but I'm pretty sure you got better grades than I did in high school."

"Better than your sister, too." Carolyn was a year ahead of him. "But she went off to a fancy college back east. I could only take part-time classes at Mesa State. Then I couldn't even afford that. I had to drop out."

"That's rough."

"I could have gotten one of those scholarships your family set up for kids in our area, but I never even applied. My daddy said that we didn't need the leftovers from the Carlisle table. I didn't need to humble myself and beg from the likes of you."

The legacy of revenge had been passed down from father to son. Trying to establish the rapport he needed, Dylan asked, "What did you study at college?"

"Shut up, Dylan. I'm not your friend." The anger returned to Nate's voice. "I never had a chance at school. Had to come home and work the operations at the Circle M."

And he blamed Dylan's family for causing him to lose his property. Better not to dwell on that. "You're a smart guy, Nate. And independent. You make your own decisions. Always have."

"Don't flatter me. I know what you really think."

He sounded cocky—as if he'd pulled off some kind of clever trick instead of this craven act of cowardice. Was it possible that he didn't see the wrong in what he was doing? What kind of heartless dog kidnapped and terrorized women? Nate was so blinded by revenge that he'd lost all sense of decency.

But Dylan couldn't allow himself to react. He had to keep the hostility from his voice, and that was something he knew how to do. He'd spent a lifetime learning how to control his emotions. When you get thrown from a horse, you don't let anybody see how much it hurts. When you lose at poker, you lay down your cards and walk away. A cowboy never wept. Nor did he break into rage. *Control.* He had to maintain control. As long as he didn't look across the table at his wife and see the raw terror in her face, he could handle this.

"I'm asking you, Nate." His voice was low, cool, monotone. "Let me talk to Maud."

"Nicole's mother. Didn't that turn out to be a big, fat surprise?" Nate gave a raspy chuckle. "When I read that journal, I couldn't hardly believe it. It was like Santa Claus dropped a present on my lap."

"A present?" *You sick bastard.* "Why do you think that?"

"Because I know you. The Carlisles will do anything to protect their family. Now that family includes Maud."

"Only if she's still alive. Let me talk to her."

There were scuffling noises, and Dylan didn't want to imagine what was going on. Then he heard Maud's voice.

"Dylan? I'm okay. I'm not hurt, just shaken up."

"That's good to know," he said. "This is going to turn

out all right, Maud. I promise. We'll do whatever necessary to get you back in one piece."

"How's Nicole?" Her voice trembled.

"She loves you."

"Enough!" Nate was back. "Here's how this is going to work, Dylan. You and Nicole get back in your car. Drive to the hot springs caves. Not the big one by the Lodge. A smaller operation that's farther west. It's called Vapor Caves."

"I want to leave Nicole out of this," Dylan said.

"And I want my ranch back. I want my herd. I want my son to live with me so I can raise him. But that's not going to happen, is it?"

"We can work out a deal." He needed to stall. Burke and Jesse would be arriving soon. "I could set you up with five hundred head of Black Angus cattle."

There was silence on the other end of the line, and Dylan knew he'd hit a nerve. Underneath all his scheming, Nate was still a rancher. He wanted that life, longed for it. Even if logic told him that he'd be arrested for kidnapping and for the murder of Lucas Mann, Nate couldn't help hoping.

And Dylan played on that slender hope. He sweetened the deal, "I can deed you the south field bordering the Grant place. We've already planted winter wheat. You'd be all set for spring."

"Why would you lift a finger to help me?"

"You and I are more alike than you think." Dylan sidestepped the obvious difference: Nate was insane. "We can work together. We can come to an agreement."

"You got fifteen minutes to get to the parking lot outside the Vapor Caves. I'll call when I know you're there. Both you and Nicole."

Still, Dylan tried to bargain. "Come on, Nate. You don't need her there."

"Maybe not." Nate's voice was flat and cold. "You can leave her behind—all alone and unprotected. Your little wife learned how to obey my instructions."

Powerful emotions surged inside Dylan, making it impossible to think or to speak. He wanted Nate Miller dead, wanted to strangle him with his bare hands and feel his wretched life slipping away.

Nate continued, "I'm guessing that Nicole would do just about anything to save her mama."

Dylan forced himself to respond. "We'll go to the Vapor Caves. Both of us."

"You're learning, Dylan. You have to do what I say."

"But we can't make it there in fifteen minutes. Give us a half hour?"

"I don't have to give you a damn thing. Be there in fifteen minutes. Or Maud is a dead woman."

Nate hung up.

Dylan had no choice but to obey.

WITH HER FINGERS CLENCHED on the steering wheel, Nicole drove their rental SUV toward the meeting place. Her nerves were strung as tight as a barbed-wire fence. Sure, she was scared. But not terrified.

Because she wasn't alone. Dylan stood with her— supporting and protecting her. Together, she felt that they could handle just about anything.

He sat in the passenger seat, talking on his cell phone to Burke, who had already said that he and Jesse were close. They'd passed Rifle and Silt—less than twenty miles away on the highway. They'd be here in less than a half hour, but it wasn't going to be soon enough.

As Nicole drove into the empty parking area, Dylan gave Burke the location of the Vapor Caves. A couple of inches of snow had accumulated on the pavement, and Nicole saw tire tracks from other vehicles. Other cars had been here and left.

An A-frame house butted up to the rocky hillside, which was dotted with scraggly, snow-covered pine trees. A worn, wooden sign over the door read: Vapor Caves. Nature's Greatest Wonder. Other signs advertised massage and spa treatments. This was a much smaller operation than the Yampah Caves near the Lodge and definitely not first-class.

She pulled up near the door and left the car idling, ready to drive away fast if necessary. "Why isn't anyone here?"

"There's a note on the door." He squinted through the windshield. "Closed for repairs."

She checked the rearview mirrors. "I don't see Nate. Did we get here on time?"

"We made it with two minutes to spare." He reached over and touched her shoulder. "I meant what I said to Maud. I won't let him hurt her."

"He already has." Nicole knew firsthand what it felt like to be abducted and held. It pained her to think of Maud in the same situation. "We can't guarantee that she'll be safe. Not while Nate's in control."

"But we're going to do everything we can to rescue her, and we've got to believe that it's going to work out. That's how we do our business. Always plan for the best."

"But prepare for the worst."

She'd heard him say that a thousand times. He applied that rule to everything from the purchase of a new vehicle to the vagaries of weather. In this case, the worst was unthinkable.

She tried to stop her mind from going there. Nate had already killed Lucas. *Poor Lucas!* His ashes were still in her suitcase in the back of the car. She wanted justice for him.

"Look at me, darlin'."

Stiffly, her head turned toward him. In spite of their dire situation, his green eyes shone with a clear, steady light. He radiated confidence and strength. This was the man she loved, the man she was meant to be with for the rest of her life, the father of her baby. They had everything to live for.

"I'm scared," she admitted.

"So am I."

"You don't look it."

"Hey, I'm good at keeping my feelings inside. Remember?"

"Of course I remember. Haven't I jumped all over you for not sharing your emotions?"

A wide grin spread across his face. "I like that image. Having you jump all over me."

She couldn't believe his mind had gone down that path. "Please don't tell me you're thinking about sex."

"Always."

"We're in a life-or-death situation. Literally. And you're having sex fantasies?"

"Darlin', that's my reason to go on living."

In spite of her rising fear, she laughed. "Not the only reason, I hope."

"I can think of a few other things."

Her cell phone rang, and she jumped. Negotiations for Maud's safety were about to start. When Dylan took the call, she was hugely relieved. She still didn't trust herself when it came to dealing with Nate.

After only a minute, he disconnected and turned to her. "Nate wants us to go inside the caves and wait for him."

"He could already be in there, waiting to ambush us."

"I don't think so," Dylan said. "I seriously doubt a cell phone will work inside the cave, which means we won't have any way to communicate with Burke."

"That was probably Nate's plan. To cut us off from any possible backup."

"And there's another problem," he said. "I was hoping I could send you on your way and take care of this by myself. But I can't leave you unprotected while Nate approaches."

*As if I'd stay behind?* "We're a team. For better or worse." *Until death us do part.*

As they walked toward the A-frame, gusts of wind swirled the light snow around them. The icy flakes burned on her cheeks. The entrance to the A-frame office was unlocked, and they went inside.

A scratched wood counter stretched across the front. The carpet showed signs of wear. A couple of chairs and a table were arranged around a freestanding fireplace that needed cleaning. Definitely not a high-class establishment.

Dylan went to the front window and peered out. "Nate said we should wait for him inside the caves."

She prowled toward the rear of the office. On either side, there were dressing rooms for men and women. A sign over a door at the rear pointed the entrance to the caves. "It's back here."

She glanced into the women's dressing room where a couple of terrycloth robes hung from pegs. Towels were stacked on a wood bench by the door. The tile floor could have used a good scrubbing. Not exactly the most sanitary conditions. If she'd been coming here for a spa treatment, she would have been uncomfortable stripping down to her bathing suit.

She returned to the front where Dylan was still at the window. He checked his wristwatch. "Burke should be here any minute."

"He won't do anything to spook Nate, will he?"

"We talked about that on the phone. He understands that Maud is a hostage. Her safety comes first."

She wasn't convinced. "Are you sure?"

"He's FBI. He knows how to deal with hostage situations. And he's got even more motivation than that. If he messes up, he'll have to face the wrath of Carolyn."

She went to the front counter and shuffled through the papers stacked by the phone. Several phone messages referred to a problem with the electricity. She found Nate's business card, advertising his experience as a handyman. "I think I know why this place is closed."

Dylan glanced over his shoulder. "Why?"

"Nate's business card is right here. He probably messed with their electricity, then showed up to fix it."

"From the looks of this place," Dylan said, "all he needed to do to be hired was offer a cheap rate."

That must have been how he'd set this trap. "So he's familiar with the set-up here."

"And the electrical system. The lights are on right now, but Nate could have them rigged to go dark. See if you can find flashlights and matches. Anything that might be useful in the caves."

Quickly, she gathered up supplies from behind the

desk. Rubber bands, a ball of twine, two flashlights, a pocket knife with a dull blade.

"He's here," Dylan said.

She joined him at the window. "He's using Maud's van."

"Burke said it was missing from her house."

Nate disappeared around the back of the van. When he stepped out and came toward them, he was holding Maud with one arm around her waist. In his other hand was a gun pointed to Maud's head.

Nicole's heart sank as she saw her dear friend—her birth mother—being treated so cruelly. "We have to do what he said. He'll kill her."

Dylan took her hand. Together, they walked through the entrance into the caves.

# Chapter Twenty-One

Even before her kidnapping, Nicole hadn't liked being in enclosed spaces. The door from the office opened into a narrow passage with five carved stone steps leading to the key-shaped opening of the cave. She clung to the railing fastened to the limestone wall. The only illumination came from a string of bare lightbulbs.

Less claustrophobic was the actual cave—not exactly spacious, probably thirty feet by fifty with benches lining the walls. The ceiling arched twenty feet high. She took a breath and concentrated on the space instead of the stone. The last thing she needed was another reason to be afraid.

"Kind of pretty," Dylan said. "In a prehistoric way."

"The minerals in the water vapor are supposed to be good for you." Her voice echoed slightly. "That's what the brochure said."

"Look around. Make it fast."

She paced along the right wall. The heat overwhelmed her. She'd seen a sign in the front office saying it was one hundred and ten degrees in the cave. Stifling hot, the vaporous air smelled of the natural minerals from the hot springs.

Dylan sniffed the mist. "Sulfur."

"And something metallic." It felt as though they'd entered the bowels of hell. Instead of facing demons with pitchforks, Nate was coming for them. "How are we going to get out of here?"

"Don't know."

He peeled off his jacket and tossed it on a bench. She did the same but clung to her purse, which was loaded with her gun and the other implements she'd gathered in the office, including the flashlight. Gingerly, she circled all the way around the cave. In the silence, she could hear the spring waters rushing behind the walls. Woven mats covered much of the floor, and she guessed that the bare stone beneath the mats would be slippery. Moisture glistened everywhere.

Dylan ducked into a smaller cave that branched off from the main room. "It's even hotter in here. There doesn't seem to be another way out."

No escape. No exit.

Dylan took her into the smaller cave. "I want you to stay back here. Have your gun ready."

She'd begun to sweat. The heat was making her dizzy. "What should I be ready for?"

"There are two of us and only one of him," he said. "He'll have to come through the same entrance we used. I'll try to get Maud away from him. If you have a clear shot, take it."

"You want me to shoot Nate?"

"I'm hoping I can get the drop on him." He mopped the sweat from his forehead. "But if I can't…"

"It's up to me."

She didn't know if she was capable of killing another human being, but now wasn't the time for ethical questions. *Shoot first and worry about it later.* Their survival—the survival of the baby growing within her—depended on her ability to act. She sure as hell wasn't going to wimp out. She took the gun from her purse.

Dylan's grin was even hotter than vapors. "I love you, darlin'. We're going to be okay."

Her confidence rose to match his. "I know we are."

"If we weren't already married," he said, "I'd ask you again."

"Your timing sucks."

"Would you say yes?"

Her mind flashed on a series of arguments: The way he never listened, his focus on work instead of her and his tightly controlled emotions. They'd already dealt with many of her problems, but one issue stood out—the only issue that really mattered. Did he want a baby? Was he ready to be a father?

"Ask me again," she said, "when we get out of here."

"You're giving me a reason to get this over with."

"Good."

She fired off a quick prayer. *Please, let me walk from this cave with my husband and Maud beside me. Please, let us survive.*

"Stay low," Dylan advised. "If there's shooting, duck down and keep moving."

Leaving her inside the smaller cave, he went toward the entrance. Bending down, he lifted the edge of a woven mat. It was the size of a small area rug and moved easily. Dylan piled two of them in front of the entrance, leaving the center floor bare.

The door from the office creaked open. She heard Nate's voice. "Dylan. You down there?"

"I'm here."

"And Nicole."

"Yes."

Dylan positioned himself at the wall beside the entrance, ready to grab Nate as soon as he appeared. In his right hand he held his gun.

Then the lights went out.

DYLAN CURSED under his breath. He expected Nate to pull a trick like this. On the desk in the office, there had been notes about the electricity. Nate had planned this blackout. The son of a bitch was probably wearing the same kind of night-vision goggles that Burke carried around in his saddlebag.

"Nicole," he whispered. "You have a flashlight?"

"Should I turn it on?"

"Not yet."

"When?"

"I'll tell you."

He heard the door from the office slam shut. The darkness was impenetrable. He'd let Nate think he had the advantage.

"Hey," Dylan called out. "Is Maud with you?"

"She is," Nate said. "I promised that if you did as I said, she'd be returned to you, unhurt."

"Prove it," he demanded. "I want to hear her voice."

There sounds of a scuffle, then a loud gasp.

"I'm right here," Maud said. "Nate's holding on to me. Can't see a thing, but I think we're going down some stairs."

*Good job, Maud. Keep talking.* "Are you okay?"

"As good as I can be with my hands tied in front of me," she said. Another useful bit of information. "At least he untied my ankles."

"Shut up," Nate growled.

Dylan formed a mental picture of Nate coming down the five stairs, holding Maud in front of him. There would be no way to get a clean shot at him without hitting her. He slipped his gun back into the holster, leaving both his hands free.

Blinded by darkness, he had to rely on his other senses. Damn, it was hot in here. When he touched the stone wall beside the cave entrance, he wasn't sure if he was feeling moisture from the vapors or his own sweat.

He listened for the sound of their footfalls. As soon as they entered the cave, he'd have to act fast.

"No sudden moves," Nate warned. "I'm holding a gun to Maud's head. It'd be a shame if my trigger finger slipped."

Not wanting to betray his position, Dylan said nothing. He noticed that Nicole was silent, too. And he hoped she had the good sense to stay hidden in the second cave.

Dylan's first move would be to yank Nate's gun arm down and shove Maud out of the way. Then he'd make a grab for the night-vision goggles.

Hoping to misdirect Nate's attention, he took his cell phone from his pocket and lobbed it toward the other side of the cave, where it clattered against the stone wall.

"Slow down," Maud said. "I can't see a damn thing."

Her voice was close. She and Nate were almost to the entrance. Dylan timed his move, acting before Nate saw him.

His left arm arced forward, coming into contact with Nate's shoulder. At the same time, Maud let out a shriek. She must have tripped over the mats he'd piled near the entrance.

With his left hand, Dylan grasped Nate's arm, pulled it down toward the floor. A gunshot exploded.

"Get out of the way, Maud."

Dylan swung blindly toward Nate's head. He'd been right about the night goggles. He struggled with the strap that circled Nate's head, trying to pull off the goggles. With his other hand, he fought for the gun.

In the dark he lost his grasp on the goggles. If Nate got away from him, it was game over. He kept hold of Nate's arm. The gun went off again.

Dylan called to Nicole. "Now. I need light."

"I'm trying. It doesn't work."

In spite of his efforts, Nate still had his goggles. One hell of a big advantage. He could see, while Dylan was blind. He swung Nate around. Together they crashed into a wall. And Dylan lost his grasp.

Nate slithered away from him.

Dylan pulled his gun from the holster and dropped to one knee on the hard stone floor of the cave. He couldn't aim, couldn't shoot. His bullet might hit either Maud or Nicole. The hot vapors wrapped around him. Sweat ran down his face in rivulets. He heard Nate laugh and tried to figure out where the sound was coming from.

"You almost had me," Nate said. "Too bad you couldn't hold on."

Though he couldn't see a damn thing, Dylan squinted. "Let's talk. We can make a deal."

"These night-vision goggles do a good job. I can see all three of you."

"Let the women go. This is between you and me."

"I want my full measure of revenge," Nate said. "Because of you, I lost my ranch. And my wife left me. Seems only right that you should lose your pretty little wife."

He meant to kill her. Dylan's worst nightmare. He'd rather die a thousand times than to have her injured.

Nicole's voice echoed in the darkness. "Go to hell, Nate."

"Stand still," he ordered her. "Quit moving around."

"You don't tell me what to do," she said. "Not ever again. You're nothing. Nobody."

"Since when did you get so tough?"

"You deserved every bad thing that happened to you," she said. "You're weak and mean."

Nate laughed. "I see you. You can't hide from me." Another laugh. "Hey, Dylan. I'm raising my gun. Pointing it at your wife. Say goodbye."

Finally the beam of Nicole's flashlight cut through the darkness. Like a desperate firefly, it circled the cave. And the light came to rest on Nate.

Dylan fired twice. The flashlight remained steady on Nate as his knees folded. He collapsed facedown on the floor of the cave. In a few steps, Dylan was on him. He kicked the gun away from Nate's hand and felt for a pulse.

"Is he dead?" Nicole asked.

"Not yet."

"Well," Maud said, "that's too bad."

The door from the office swung open, spilling light down the stairs. Burke called out, "FBI."

"You can put your guns away," Dylan said. "And call for an ambulance."

"We could give him first aid," Maud said. "But I don't like to handle venomous creatures."

Dylan gathered his wife into his arms. "You did it."

"We did it together. We're a team."

Meant to be together. For better or worse.

NICOLE BARELY had a chance to catch her breath. The ambulance arrived first. Two EMTs loaded Nate onto a stretcher, carried him up from the cave and drove away. A third paramedic stayed behind to provide first aid for Maud and Dylan, both of whom insisted they were all right and would not require hospitalization. Then came the Glenwood Springs police and the Garfield County Sheriff. The interior of the A-frame office was packed with lawmen, flashing credentials and asking questions.

Nicole found a relatively quiet corner near the unlit fireplace. After being in the super-heated cave, the cool temperature felt good. Maud stood beside her.

Gently, Nicole took Maud's hand. "I should have guessed."

"And I should have said something." Maud's blue eyes—the same shade as Nicole's—shone brightly. "I didn't want to mess up your life. If you had wanted to find your birth mother, I would have stepped forward. But you never looked."

"I loved my parents." She hadn't felt the need to search for anyone else. "I never forgot that I was adopted. That's part of who I am. But I felt lucky that my parents wanted me. Really wanted me."

"They were good people." Maud chewed her lower lip—a nervous habit that Nicole had, as well. "Is there anything you want to ask me?"

"One question. Why did you give me up?"

"I was only sixteen when I had you. Your biological father was out of the picture, and I knew I was too immature to raise a child. The adoption people took you from me in the hospital, but I never forgot you. And I never ever stopped loving you."

"When you moved to Rawlins…"

"I was looking for you," Maud said. "Don't get me wrong. I'm not a stalker. There were plenty of other reasons to stay in Rawlins. It's a great little town, and my vet practice did really well. I sold it for a pretty penny before I moved to Delta. Being near you was the icing on the cake."

"You were always there," Nicole said. "At church. At the rodeos."

"Keep in mind that I was only in my early thirties then. I fully expected to find a man, get married and have other kids. Then, there was the accident. And the hysterectomy." A tear slipped down her cheek. "You visited me in the hospital."

"I loved you as a friend and a mentor." With her thumb, Nicole brushed away the tear. "And I still love you, Mom."

They held each other for a long moment.

Ever since her parents had died, there had been a gap in Nicole's heart. Dylan's family and the hands at the ranch, like Lucas, could do only so much to fill that empty space. Embracing Maud—her birth mother—fulfilled her need for family. A need she hadn't even been aware of. And when she told Maud about the baby…

Her gaze lit on Dylan. Standing beside Jesse, her husband looked battered around the edges. Streaks of grime from the cave marked his cheeks and jaw. The paramedics had applied a bandage to his left hand where he'd been injured in his struggle with Nate. His jeans were torn at the knee.

But Jesse and Burke had brought his favorite hat. As soon as Dylan put it on, he became a cowboy. The owner of the Carlisle ranch. The man she loved.

Separating from Maud, she said, "I need to talk to Dylan."

"I'll be here."

"You always were." Nicole squeezed her hand. She couldn't ask for a more attentive friend or a wiser mentor.

Dylan must have sensed her moving toward him, because he turned to face her. In spite of everything else that was happening in the A-frame office, he focused solely on her. He grasped her hand. "Come outside with me."

"It's still snowing."

"And mercifully cold," he said. "I feel like I've been parboiled from that cave."

She slipped on her jacket and went with him. They strolled through lightly falling snow to the side of the A-frame where they could have privacy.

"In the cave," he said, "I asked you a question."

"Not yet." She placed her hand on his chest. "There's something I have to tell you first."

"Okay, darlin'. I'm listening."

She could tell that he truly was paying full attention. "We have a new member in our family."

"Maud," he said.

"Yes." She swallowed hard. He'd seemed so resistant to the idea of having children. How would he react? "And there's another. Dylan, I'm pregnant."

He drew back, as if her announcement had physically smacked him in the jaw. "We're having a baby."

"Yes."

"You're sure?"

"When Doctor Sarah did blood tests on me, she found out."

He went silent, and her heart sank. This was a mistake. She should have known. His resistance with the fertility doctors should have been a clue.

"In my whole life," he said, "I've never been so scared. What if I make mistakes? What if I'm not a good dad?"

"You will be," she said.

Tears spilled down his cheeks. The cowboy who never showed emotion was weeping openly. "This is more than I ever hoped for. A baby. A precious little baby."

"Our baby."

He threw back his head and gave a whoop, tore off his hat and threw it in the air. After a crazy jig, he grabbed her and danced her around the parking lot.

"I promise you, darlin', I'm going try my best. Not going to be like my dad. I'm going to love you and our baby."

"I love you." She grabbed him and kissed him hard. "I never thought you'd be so happy."

"Neither did I," he said. "But, damn!"

His antics had drawn the attention of the others who poured out of the A-frame. Jesse said, "What the hell's going on?"

"We're pregnant," Dylan yelled.

He whirled and dropped to one knee before her. "Nicole, my love, will you marry me? Again."

"Yes. As many times as you want."

The watchers near the A-frame let out a cheer. They were slapping each other on the back, laughing and grinning. Everyone was full of cheer.

This was going to be the best Christmas ever.

# Epilogue

Eight months later, Nicole stood at the back of the lavishly decorated church in Denver. Originally, Carolyn had planned for a June wedding, but this extravaganza had required an extra two months of preparation. There were over four hundred guests, including the Mayor and the Governor.

Nicole's maid-of-honor dress had been altered three times to accommodate her growing pregnancy. In the dark purple gown, she felt like a walking eggplant. Beside her, Fiona Grant—one of five bridesmaids—was slim and delicate in the same style.

Two months ago, Fiona and Jesse Longbridge had been married in a quiet ceremony on the ranch. Jesse had quit the security business and was working full-time as the foreman for Carlisle Certified Organic Beef. He and Dylan had bonded like brothers, and Nicole was delighted that Dylan was willing to hand off some of his responsibilities to Jesse.

Fiona whispered, "There must be a thousand purple gladioli in here. And a million miles of satin ribbon."

"Subtle, huh?" Nicole rested her hand on her belly. The baby was kicking again. An active little rascal.

"Dylan and I still can't figure out what to give Carolyn and Burke for a wedding present. A gravy boat just doesn't seem like enough."

"Maybe a gravy yacht," Fiona suggested.

"I know what your present will be. One of your custom-made pottery pieces. A Navajo wedding vase?"

"In purple," Fiona said. "I'd like to make one for you and Dylan. I heard you're going to renew your vows."

"After the baby's born."

There wasn't a rush. She'd never felt so very married and so very happy.

As the organist launched into "The Wedding March," Jesse and Dylan—both looking dashing in tuxedos—stepped up to escort their ladies down the aisle.

Dylan leaned down to kiss her behind the ear. "Today, you're not the bride," he whispered.

"I know."

"But you're still the most beautiful woman in the room."

Of course, she didn't believe him. But when she looked into his eyes and saw their love reflected, she knew he was telling the truth. "If that's the way you see it…"

"I do," he said.

"I do, too."

Halfway down the aisle, Nicole's water broke.

Carolyn was going to be furious.

\* \* \* \* \*

\* \* \*

'THIS EVENING I'm flying to New York for two weeks,'
Jasim imparted with a casualness that made her heart sink
like a stone. 'That's why I had you brought here. I own this
apartment and you'll be comfortable here while I'm abroad.'

'I can afford my own accommodation although I may not
need it for long. I'll have another job by the time you
get back—'

Jasim released a slightly harsh laugh. 'There's no need for
you to look for another position. How would I ever see you?
Don't you understand what I'm offering you?'

Elinor stood very still. 'No, I must be incredibly thick
because I haven't quite worked out yet what you're offering
me.…'

His charismatic smile slashed his lean dark visage.
'Naturally, I want to take care of you.…'

'No, thanks.' Elinor forced a smile and mentally willed him not to demean her with some sordid proposition. 'The only man who will ever take *care* of me with my agreement will be my husband. I'm willing to wait for you to come back but I'm not willing to be kept by you. I'm a very independent woman and what I give, I give freely.'

Jasim frowned. 'You make it all sound so serious.'

'What happened between us last night left pure chaos in its wake. Right now, I don't know whether I'm on my head or my heels. I'll stay for a while because I have nowhere else to go in the short term. So maybe it's good that you'll be away for a while.'

Jasim pulled out his wallet to extract a card. 'My private number,' he told her, presenting her with it as though it was a precious gift, which indeed it was. Many women would have done just about anything to gain access to that direct hotline to him, but his staff guarded his privacy with scrupulous care.

Before he could close the wallet, his blood ran cold in his veins. How could he have made such a serious oversight? What if he had got her pregnant? He knew that an unplanned pregnancy would engulf his life like an avalanche, crush his freedom and suffocate him. He barely stilled a shudder at the threat of such an outcome and thought how ironic it was that what his older brother had longed and prayed for to secure the line to the throne should strike Jasim as an absolute disaster....

\* \* \*

*What will proud Prince Jasim do if Elinor is expecting his royal baby? Perhaps an arranged marriage is the only solution! But will Elinor agree? Find out in DESERT PRINCE, BRIDE OF INNOCENCE by Lynne Graham [#2884], available from Harlequin Presents® in January 2010.*

HPEX0110B

HARLEQUIN *Presents*

Bestselling Harlequin Presents author

# Lynne Graham

brings you an exciting new miniseries:

PREGNANT BRIDES

*Inexperienced and expecting, they're forced to marry*

Collect them all:

## DESERT PRINCE, BRIDE OF INNOCENCE

*January 2010*

## RUTHLESS MAGNATE, CONVENIENT WIFE

*February 2010*

## GREEK TYCOON, INEXPERIENCED MISTRESS

*March 2010*

**www.eHarlequin.com**

## New Year, New Man!

*For the perfect New Year's punch,*
*blend the following:*

- *One woman determined to find her inner vixen*
- *A notorious—and notoriously hot!—playboy*
- *A provocative New Year's Eve bash*
- *An impulsive kiss that leads to a night of*
  *explosive passion!*

When the clock hits midnight Claire Daniels
kisses the guy standing closest to her, but
the kiss doesn't end after the bells stop ringing....

## Look for

# Moonstruck

## by *USA TODAY* bestselling author
# JULIE KENNER

*Available January*

---

# red-hot reads

www.eHarlequin.com

HB79518

# REQUEST YOUR FREE BOOKS!

## 2 FREE NOVELS
## PLUS 2
## FREE GIFTS!

◆ HARLEQUIN®

# INTRIGUE®

## Breathtaking Romantic Suspense

**YES!** Please send me 2 FREE Harlequin Intrigue® novels and my 2 FREE gifts (gifts are worth about $10). After receiving them, if I don't wish to receive any more books, I can return the shipping statement marked "cancel." If I don't cancel, I will receive 6 brand-new novels every month and be billed just $4.24 per book in the U.S. or $4.99 per book in Canada. That's a savings of close to 15% off the cover price! It's quite a bargain! Shipping and handling is just 50¢ per book.* I understand that accepting the 2 free books and gifts places me under no obligation to buy anything. I can always return a shipment and cancel at any time. Even if I never buy another book from Harlequin, the two free books and gifts are mine to keep forever.

182 HDN EYTR   382 HDN EYT3

| Name | (PLEASE PRINT) | |
|------|------|------|
| Address | | Apt. # |
| City | State/Prov. | Zip/Postal Code |

Signature (if under 18, a parent or guardian must sign)

### Mail to the **Harlequin Reader Service:**
**IN U.S.A.:** P.O. Box 1867, Buffalo, NY 14240-1867
**IN CANADA:** P.O. Box 609, Fort Erie, Ontario L2A 5X3

Not valid to current subscribers of Harlequin Intrigue books.

**Are you a current subscriber of Harlequin Intrigue books
and want to receive the larger-print edition?
Call 1-800-873-8635 today!**

* Terms and prices subject to change without notice. Prices do not include applicable taxes. Sales tax applicable in N.Y. Canadian residents will be charged applicable provincial taxes and GST. Offer not valid in Quebec. This offer is limited to one order per household. All orders subject to approval. Credit or debit balances in a customer's account(s) may be offset by any other outstanding balance owed by or to the customer. Please allow 4 to 6 weeks for delivery. Offer available while quantities last.

**Your Privacy:** Harlequin is committed to protecting your privacy. Our Privacy Policy is available online at www.eHarlequin.com or upon request from the Reader Service. From time to time we make our lists of customers available to reputable third parties who may have a product or service of interest to you. If you would prefer we not share your name and address, please check here. ☐

HI09R

*From glass slippers to silk sheets*

Once upon a time there was a humble housekeeper.
Proud but poor, she went to work for a charming and
ruthless rich man!

She thought her place was below stairs—
but her gorgeous boss had other ideas.

Her place was in the bedroom, between his
luxurious silk sheets.

Stripped of her threadbare uniform, buxom and blushing
in his bed, she'll discover that a woman's work has never
been so much fun!

Look out for:

# POWERFUL ITALIAN, PENNILESS HOUSEKEEPER

*by India Grey*
#2886
*Available January 2010*

www.eHarlequin.com

HP12886

 HARLEQUIN®

# INTRIGUE®

## COMING NEXT MONTH

### Available January 12, 2010

**#1179 THE SOCIALITE AND THE BODYGUARD
by Dana Marton**
*Bodyguard of the Month*
The ex-commando bodyguard couldn't believe his luck when he was assigned to protect a socialite's poodle. But as he learns that opposites really can attract, he also realizes that his socialite may be the real target of the death threats....

**#1180 CLASSIFIED COWBOY by Mallory Kane**
*The Silver Star of Texas: Comanche Creek*
The forensic anthropologist had caught the Texas Ranger's eye years ago, and now he's back for a second chance at love—and at cracking an old case.

**#1181 THE SHADOW by Aimée Thurlo**
*Brotherhood of Warriors*
After a series of incidents and threats puts her project—and her life—in jeopardy, she has no choice but to depend on the ex-army ranger to protect her.

**#1182 A PERFECT STRANGER by Jenna Ryan**
On the run, her new life is put in danger when a gorgeous ex-cop tracks her down and unknowingly exposes her. His conscience won't let him abandon her, and their attraction can only grow stronger... if they survive.

**#1183 CASE FILE: CANYON CREEK, WYOMING
by Paula Graves**
*Cooper Justice*
After almost falling victim to a killer, she's the only one who can help a determined Wyoming officer bring him to justice.

**#1184 THE SHERIFF OF SILVERHILL by Carol Ericson**
The FBI agent returns home to investigate a serial killer, only to find that the sheriff she's working with is the man she had to leave behind.